SOULDEATH

J. THOMPSON

Copyright © 2017 J Thompson all rights reserved. No part of this book may be used or reproduced in any manner whatsoever without written permission from the author except in the case of brief quotations embodied in articles and reviews.

This edition is published by J Thompson

This book is sold subject to the condition that it shall not, by way of trade or otherwise, be lent, resold, hired out or otherwise circulated without the prior consent of the publisher in any form of binding or cover other than that in which it is published and without a similar condition including this condition being imposed on the subsequent purchaser.

This is a work of fiction. Names, characters, places and incidents are the product of the author's imagination and are used fictitiously. Any resemblance to actual persons, living or dead, business establishments, events or locales is entirely coincidental.

Front Cover Designed by Jada D'Lee Designs
www.jadadleedesigns.com

Editor. Elaine Wilson. Elisia Goodman

Contents

A conflicted god	v
Prologue	1
Chapter 1	11
Chapter 2	23
Chapter 3	29
Chapter 4	43
Chapter 5	53
Chapter 6	63
Chapter 7	79
Chapter 8	85
Chapter 9	97
Chapter 10	103
Chapter 11	117
Chapter 12	125
Chapter 13	135
Chapter 14	141
Chapter 15	153
Chapter 16	157
Chapter 17	163
Chapter 18	173
Chapter 19	181
Chapter 20	191
Chapter 21	199
Chapter 22	205
Chapter 23	215
Chapter 24	221

Chapter 25	229
Chapter 26	237
Chapter 27	243
Chapter 28	249
Epilogue	253
Acknowledgments	261
A Note From Jenn	263

From Soulfate

A Conflicted God

The bright blue shimmering liquid glimmered in the pale light that filled the throne room of Hades' immense stone temple. Sconces burst with flame and caused shadows to pulse and then retreat back against the marble columns. Hades himself sat within the quiet of the room, slouched on his throne. He had one foot rested upon the knee of the other leg, his elbows stretched out onto the arms of the chair, and in his right hand he held a bottle that contained the blue liquid.

Hades, god and lord of the underworld, was confused and irritable. For the first time in his long existence, he didn't know how to proceed. The bottle he held within his hands was the love potion he had fairly won from Aphrodite herself, but he was loath to use it. To force someone to feel what they could possibly never feel on their own ate at his soul.

The reputation of the gods was a harsh one - they were known for not caring about anything but themselves - but as with most things in life, what had been said wasn't necessarily right. Hades cared - you could say he cared too much - and that was, in part, what caused his current irritability.

He eyed the bottle one more time and then leaned his head back against the headrest of his throne and closed his eyes. He would not use the potion, but he would have Aphrodite help him, and if she was to deny him that request, he would be forced to use blackmail. He had, after all, helped bring her back from the brink of death and aided the mortals she was so fond of. He had even addressed the balance and helped the warrior, Cosmos. The warrior had made the sacrifice and closed the portal his father Apollo had created by using his own blood and that of Apollo. In doing this he had sealed the creatures back onto their plain of Tartarus and severed all ties with the goddess and the oracle.

This alone had earned him a boon, and as he had so obviously fallen for the oracle he was protecting, Hades had decided to give him the happy ever after most mortals don't get. Hades smirked to himself, he had left Apollo trapped as a sort of penance for his misdeeds and, in short, causing a bloody uproar. He had messed with the energies of Olympus herself, and as such, Zeus had vanished in the hopes he could sort the issue.

Hades opened his eyes and looked at the richly

decorated ceiling of the temple. An exact replica of the night's sky had been painted, the stars created from crystals sparkled from their constellations. But the beauty felt wasted, it demanded more than his own perusal. With a heavy sigh, he sat up then got to his feet, where he stretched his muscled form. The dark toga effortlessly hung to him and showcased his strength.

He would gain the goddess's help, and maybe then his heart would finally get what it had been pining for.

Love. Even the gods coveted it.

Prologue

DEATH, A NEW START

Death: not as cold or as frightening as some would expect or believe. No longer weighed down with the pain and emotions of her mortal life, Airlea finally felt free.

With a calm detachment, she looked down upon the still form of her body. She expected to feel some sort of calmness or even regret, but as she looked closer, she was quickly reminded of the hell her life had been.

Her face held a serenity that belied the trauma that had been subjected to her slight body. She sighed, but no breath left her lips. He never did go for the face. He would always hide the evidence and made sure the truth was never visible. He hid his true self; a monster, a fiend with an angel's face.

When Airlea had been promised to her husband,

she had been as excited as a future bride could be. He was a wealthy man, born of Athens, and most respected. At 16, this was the best she could hope for in life, and she had thanked the gods for her dreams coming true. She wanted to be a good wife, and if she was lucky, a good mother to many. What young girl didn't want that? Not long after their wedding, Airlea soon found the truth; marriage wasn't, in fact, the dreams and wishes people spoke of.

She reached out with a pale ghostly arm and placed her palm against the cheek of her still form. The skin blue and translucent, Airlea sighed again.

The bruises and broken bones were hidden from view yet she could still remember, with clarity, each and every feeling of hurt; each punch, every slap, and finally the feeling of cold, sharp steel as it pressed through her tender flesh, ending her short life and that of her unborn child.

Airlea had hoped that once she became pregnant, the beatings and abuse would stop and her husband's rage would become diminished.

She was wrong.

His rage had only increased, and the brutality made her beg to the gods for mercy.

The gods had listened.

Airlea had now finally been granted that wish.

Freedom and a chance to live again, if Hades, the dark god of the underworld, let her drink of the River Lethe and allow her be reborn. Her heart leapt at the thought of the elder god himself; out of all the gods, she found him the most intriguing.

In her ghostly form, Airlea frowned. She had always felt a pull toward the god of the Underworld, even now her dead pulse raced and her palms became sweaty.

Hades himself already had a connection to her soul; she could feel it.

It was time to find out why.

---

400 YEARS PAST

OLYMPUS, SEAT OF THE GODS

Hades sat on his throne that had been placed at the front of his temple that overlooked his realm. The underworld, home to the fields of Elyssia, fields of punishment, Tartarus, and much more, was his home and his charge.

His task as the lord of the underworld was simple; to house the evil souls that passed, letting them receive justice as they lived out their deathly existence in purgatory. On the flipside, Hades was able to watch the souls that were granted passage to the fields of Elyssia, a place where they were reunited with loved ones and were also give the option to be reborn.

The great god watched as a fresh influx of souls entered the fields where many waited to see if their family had joined them. Most were filled with trepidation at being in this unknown world. A world from myth and legend. It hadn't helped at all that this particular group had been greeted by the guardian himself. Cerberus had managed to escape from his leash and had bounded down upon them. If they were not already dead, Hades was positive the three-headed dog would have caused many a heart to falter. Only, if they looked closer, they would realise he wasn't the evil hellhound of legend but rather an overgrown puppy who craved love and attention. All he really wanted was a scratch behind his ears and maybe a tummy rub, but few would venture past a horrified look at the drooling jowls and sharp teeth. His barks of delight at seeing a friendly face would always be misinterpreted for aggression and would quickly send them running, not giving him the love the big, soppy oaf craved.

As with most days, the souls that were permitted onto the fields of Elyssia were greeted by Hades' staff and those relatives that had decided not to move on and be reborn. Even though death was the reason they were here, most now smiled brightly and welcomed their time in the underworld. Those that had immediately decided they wanted to go back to the mortal world were led by Hades' faithful servants towards the river Lethe. This graceful river flowed through the underworld and called to those that wanted to start a fresh, unburdened by their past mortal life. They were given the chance to be reborn and to live out a new life with no knowledge of their past. The myth of past lives stemmed from this very river and its mighty powers, but over time, this power diminishes and is how the mortals are able to gain some semblance of their past memories.

Hades let his eyes roam over the throng of souls from his perch. He was vigilant in making sure none of the damned had made it through the barrier that separated the fields of punishment and the fields of Elyssia.

It saddened the great god that mortals took their short lives for granted; most who entered the underworld died well before old age had taken hold, their life threads cut when there were still things to finish and life to experience.

Both men and women of all shapes, sizes, and

colours walked into Elyssia, bowing before him as they passed, their eyes widening only slightly when they realised the legends were, in fact, true. It wasn't a surprise to know that even though the mortals still prayed and worshiped the gods, their actual belief was wavering.

He swept his gaze once more over the small crowd, happy that all had been accounted for and would be taken to wherever they preferred to spend their time. His gaze snagged upon a bent head of ebony hair that shimmered like the wing of a raven as the starlight touched upon it, it fell straight and true down her back. But it was her eyes that had captivated him, they stopped his heart for a second and changed the course of its beat. His soul pulsed deep inside as if she had a direct link to it. He felt like her delicate hand had wrapped around it and pulled.

Turquoise orbs, almost like the Mediterranean Sea, glowed as she walked dancelike across the soft grass. Her full figure drew his gaze as he swept it across her form in a slow perusal; breasts that looked large enough to fill - if not overflow - his hands, wide, womanly hips that made him salivate.

"Fuck," Hades said through gritted teeth as he scrubbed a hand down his face, his body instantly on fire for this female. This both confused and angered him; never, in all his long existence, had he experienced a feeling like this for any woman. She was surely a siren sent to tempt and torture him.

Hades rose from his seat, and on long legs, strode towards the group of mortal souls that surrounded her. He watched them laugh easily, so at ease within his kingdom. Her smile was stunningly beautiful and alluring, and sent him off-kilter.

But he wasn't allowed to feel like this; his job was to watch over the souls, not covet them. His heart pounded so hard that he was positive the souls before him could hear it.. He was pulled to her and there was nothing he could do but follow his soul's demand.

As he approached the group, most turned and gasped. He couldn't blame them. The sight of the god of the underworld was truly awe-inspiring, if he didn't say so himself. Dressed almost entirely in a navy blue so dark it appeared black, he was a domineering figure indeed. They backed up as he approached and were quick to drop to their knees.

Were they afraid of him? Surely not.

Hades came to an abrupt stop and watched the souls carefully, not wanting to scare them anymore. Why had he ventured to them again? Oh yes, the female; he was entranced by her beauty.

"Please stand, you need not bow or kneel here in the underworld."

He smiled and looked at the souls one at a time before his eyes met with the luminous ones of the female. They locked and held. Hades' heart stalled within his chest and he struggled to take a breath. Her slight smile towards him lightened his mood and he was able to breathe again, his lips tilting up higher.

Hades placed his right fist over his heart and bowed low towards the female, his voice clear as he spoke, "My lady, I bid you welcome to Elyssia."

The female smiled again and performed a curtsey in return. When she spoke, her voice quiet yet lyrical, it affected Hades more than he was ready to admit. "Thank you, oh great lord Hades."

She was simply stunning, and she did literally take his breath away, but she was dead, merely a soul seeking refuge. Or would she seek the river Lethe and return to the mortal world?

Hades bowed again and schooled his features. "Anything you need, all of you," he looked to the now larger group of souls that surrounded him, "you have only to call. My servants will assist you with all you need."

This woman had captivated him. In fact, she had his soul. But none would know. He would seek her out as a mortal, should she be reborn, seek her out and make her his. But none of his fellow gods would know.

Hades' mood shifted and became sour. He turned with a flourish of his long, dark cloak and stalked towards his temple and away from the beauty that would remain in his mind and dreams for centuries to come.

Chapter One

THE PRESENT

Hades was pissed, actually he was more than pissed, and for the life of him he couldn't remember that mortal phrase that would sum up his current feelings. Even the term 'fucked off' couldn't cover how he felt.

The great god of the underworld finally pinned the messenger of the gods with a heavy glare. Hermes met his gaze head-on from where he sat.

"I'm sorry, but what the fuck did you just say?" Hades ground out, wanting Hermes to repeat his last words just so he could get confirmation on what a clusterfuck of a day this was turning out to be.

Hermes, always the overly cocky bastard, grinned as he leaned forward, his voice far too cheerful considering the news. "I said, oh mighty old one," he paused for effect, but all it did was make the elder god more and more annoyed, "Demeter has stated that it is now time to fulfil the bargain you made. She feels her daughter is ready."

Hades clenched his fists as his side. His knuckles cracked under the pressure and echoed throughout the temple, and Hermes flinched ever so slightly.

"As far as I am concerned, that deal was made void by the fact Persephone wanted nothing to do with me, and quite frankly, I want fuck all to do with her as well."

Hermes stood and took a step towards the brooding god. "My lord, Demeter insists and is willing to take this matter to Zeus if it is not done."

Yeah, good luck with that one, Hades thought, and stood, his long black cloak flowing out behind him as he paced across the room. Zeus had been MIA for a while now. Not that he could blame him; Hera had been on the war path lately. Hades pinned Hermes with his gaze, his dark eyes boring into the bright green of the messenger.

"So, basically, you're saying that I am now to be forced to marry an immature, dull, brainless goddess because her mother believes it will "curb her frivolous ways, teach her humility, and bring balance", because being in the underworld obviously teaches all those things." Hades spread his arms as he spoke. "Really, she thinks all that will happen with that girl in my domain only a few months out of the year. Is that right?"

"Yes, my lord. Simply put, but yes." Hermes felt for Hades. There was no denying the goddess Persephone's beauty, but she was, in short, one beer short of a six pack. She took the term ditzy to a whole new level. It also didn't help that there had been a hell of a lot of strange rumours floating around that concerned her extra goddess activities. That in itself would explain why Demeter was so keen to have her paired off with Hades.

Zeus was a known womanizer, and Poseidon just didn't give a shit – he also had his own hands full getting to grips with the product of his own 'dealings' with the mortals.

"I am not fucking marrying her, Hermes. I couldn't give a shit what Demeter has said, or my brother, for that matter."

Hermes watched as the great god paced. He found it almost entertaining that Hades, as well as Aphrodite, had started to talk more and more like a mortal, especially their swearing. Anger pulsed from the lord of the dead, and Hermes was grateful he wasn't the direct reason for the god's sour mood.

"Is that what you would like me to relay back to the goddess, my lord?"

"You can relay whatever the fuck you like, Hermes, just make sure she gets the point, the one where I am not marrying her daughter."

Hermes nodded, then stood, his gold staff gripped in his hand as he bowed. "I will take leave of you then, my lord."

"Hermes, stop being so bloody formal, it's starting to piss me off."

Hermes smirked, then inclined his head. "Looks like the mortals' way with words are becoming the norm around here."

Hades' lips tilted in a smirk of his own. "Indeed," he added as he stalked back over to his throne and sat down. "I find I prefer it."

"Well, it suits you."

The dark god let loose a full-blown smile, which was a rarity. He had become more and more sour as the years had gone by. "Ha! In the words of the mortals, I now have what you would call a potty mouth, something I am positive Demeter wouldn't like."

The lesser god laughed as he agreed, "Oh yeah, she can definitely be prissy at times." He continued to she thinks all that will happen with that girl in my domain only a few months out of the year. Is that right?"

"Yes, my lord. Simply put, but yes." Hermes felt for Hades. There was no denying the goddess Persephone's beauty, but she was, in short, one beer short of a six pack. She took the term ditzy to a whole new level. It also didn't help that there had been a hell of a lot of strange rumours floating around that concerned her extra goddess activities. That in itself would explain why Demeter was so keen to have her paired off with Hades.

Zeus was a known womanizer, and Poseidon just didn't give a shit – he also had his own hands full getting to grips with the product of his own 'dealings' with the mortals.

"I am not fucking marrying her, Hermes. I couldn't give a shit what Demeter has said, or my brother, for that matter."

Hermes watched as the great god paced. He found it almost entertaining that Hades, as well as Aphrodite, had started to talk more and more like a mortal, especially their swearing. Anger pulsed from the lord of the dead, and Hermes was grateful he wasn't the direct reason for the god's sour mood.

"Is that what you would like me to relay back to the goddess, my lord?"

"You can relay whatever the fuck you like, Hermes, just make sure she gets the point, the one where I am not marrying her daughter."

Hermes nodded, then stood, his gold staff gripped in his hand as he bowed. "I will take leave of you then, my lord."

"Hermes, stop being so bloody formal, it's starting to piss me off."

Hermes smirked, then inclined his head. "Looks like the mortals' way with words are becoming the norm around here."

Hades' lips tilted in a smirk of his own. "Indeed," he added as he stalked back over to his throne and sat down. "I find I prefer it."

"Well, it suits you."

The dark god let loose a full-blown smile, which was a rarity. He had become more and more sour as the years had gone by. "Ha! In the words of the mortals, I now have what you would call a potty mouth, something I am positive Demeter wouldn't like."

The lesser god laughed as he agreed, "Oh yeah, she can definitely be prissy at times." He continued to snigger. "Would you like me to inform the goddess of your new vocal habits?"

With a smirk, Hades nodded in response before he lost his smile, the conversation turning, once again, back to the reason for Hermes' visit and the reason why he was pissed off.

"Very well, I will do my very best to dissuade her. Do you require me for anything else?"

"No, thank you, Hermes. Good luck with your task, I don't envy you in the slightest."

With a nod, Hermes struck his staff against the marble floor, and in a bright flash, he changed into a stunning black kite. Spreading his wings, he took to the air, quickly leaving the dominion of the dead and its brooding god behind.

Hades watched as the bird vanished from sight, then sagged into his chair. The idea of being married to one of the strangest goddesses in Olympus actually made the hairs on the back of his neck stand up in warning. He had only met her once - or was it twice? - but even then, something felt off. She was stunning, but so were all the goddesses; it was the way they were made. However, there was something about Persephone that set his radar off, he could hear the warning call in his head screaming, *Danger. Danger.*

Then there was the fact that his own personal plans meant marrying her was out of the question, and they were more important to him than keeping the goddess of the harvest happy. Plans that would lead to what he hoped was a happily ever after, although they also laid on the compliance of Aphrodite. Hades had now reached breaking point - or his heart had - and the last thing he needed was the rest of Olympus knowing. So, he needed to thwart Demeter's plan for the time being until he found his soulmate, and then he would proclaim her as his queen to the rest of the gods.

His problem was he couldn't take watching her from afar anymore, and he refused to watch her soul enter the fields of Elyssia once again. She changed form each and every incarnation, so finding her was like finding the proverbial needle in a haystack. He had no doubts that he would recognise her should they meet; his soul was desperate for her. He needed to find out where she was and then do something no god before had ever had to do.

He would court her. He would charm her until she demanded to be in his arms, and then… then Hades would be the winner in this game.

Hades had observed the mortals for centuries, watched them wine and dine their females, and after seeing the warriors Arcaeus and Cosmos deal with their own, he had no doubt his chosen one would fall into his arms. *Well, who wouldn't?* he thought.

He felt a new determination sweep through him, and this made him even more eager to get his plan set in motion. Hades called out to one of his servants, his voice echoing throughout his chamber. "Send word to Aphrodite. I have need of her unique skills."

He watched the servant leave the room and smiled to himself. For once he felt a sense of hope. It was time...time for the god and lord of the dead to find his mate.

Aphrodite sipped her coffee and watched the world go by from her seat by the window. This, along with chocolate, had become one of her favourite mortal vices. She honestly wondered how the mortals could take the simple things like this for granted.

Their world had grown and come on leaps and bounds since the day the immortals had started their reign. Back then, they could openly wander amongst the mortals, but now... no one believed; not in her or her fellow immortals. No prayers were spoken or tokens left, their names were merely words in history books, only remembered now and again.

Being a goddess of Olympus had at one time meant something; there had been spectacular feasts and celebrations that both mortals and immortals attended. Now, all that was just in the past, and things on Olympus were not so rosy. Aphrodite worried for her future, as well as those of the whole pantheon. Zeus had gone away to consult with the grandmother of the new Oracle Sonia in the hopes he could learn why things had gone south. Poseidon, being the god of the sea, had become a recluse and rarely ventured out of his domain. Most had to journey to him, and even then, he wouldn't necessary see you. So that left the brooding and, at times, grumpy Hades, but even he was more approachable than Poseidon, whose domain sported the biggest *Do Not Disturb* sign ever created.

Hades was the only elder god left to help her try and figure out why things had gone wrong and what they could do to stop it. But - and it was a big but - Hades had lost focus on the bigger things, and he was now only bothered about finding his mate. Not that she blamed him, he had spent many a year watching his destined mate return to Elyssia, only to be reborn time and time again.

Aphrodite let out a deep sigh, that was a burden no one should have to deal with. The heart was strong, but to watch and know the person that held that part of him had died time and time again would break even the strongest of warriors.

"Another drink, Miss?" the cute blonde waiter asked as he took her empty cup from the table, pulling the goddess from her depressing musings.

She smiled before she answered. "Oh, yes please, sweetheart, a mocha."

Her eyes followed the young man as he went back to the bar to make her drink, and her mind once again pondered what the plan should be. There was a lot at stake, so maybe she should help Hades first, and then once he was finally happy, get his help with saving Olympus.

A cold, sharp draft swept through the room as the front door was opened. The weather had taken a turn for the chilly, and Aphrodite was glad she now wore some stunningly beautiful winter wear, thanks to her friend Sonia, who had a natural talent for choosing clothes.

The young woman who walked through the door looked to be in her mid-twenties and had long white-blonde hair that was tied back in a long braid, emphasising her ice blue eyes. She was very slight in build at only around five foot in height, but she had confidence in the way she walked.

Aphrodite smiled, and it got bigger and bigger the more she looked at the female.

Well, that had certainly been easier than she had thought it would be. Aphrodite, under the cover of her coat, waved her fingers, creating a spell that clung to the mortal. It would follow the woman wherever she went.

"Nothing wrong with a little godly stalking," she whispered as the small invisible spell took effect. The woman grabbed her take away drink and headed out the door. No one but a god would be able to see the marker the goddess had placed on the mortal, and there would be only one god that would be interested.

As the waiter set her fresh coffee down on the table, she went back to watching the world go by. Hades would be calling, sooner rather than later, and she had completed the first step in her own plan. But she wouldn't make it easy on him, he would learn the hard way and, in turn, appreciate it all the more.

Aphrodite watched people walk by, some rushing to get to their next destination, others enjoying the day, and then there were the daydreamers who smiled at nothing in particular, those were the believers, and the ones she loved to watch the most. Those still believed and would be the mortals the gods would need when the time came. They were also the souls that gave her hope that what she was doing was the right thing.

That the gods also deserved love.

And now it was Hades' turn.

Chapter Two

Andromeda tilted her head from side to side in an effort to stretch the muscles that had become stiff from staying in the same position for a while. She had been bent over her work station for well over three hours now, but every second, every minute, had been worth it. She sat back on her stool and held up the unpolished piece of silver that had taken shape.

The silver, still slightly dull from being handled, glistened slightly in the light and highlighted every detail Andromeda had worked into the metal. The round pendant was the size of her palm and was unique in every way. Inside a simple round boarder sat an elegant dragon, its style, Viking in origin, sat in a regal pose. Even unpolished and without any gems, its beauty was obvious.

Andromeda couldn't help but smile as she tilted the piece back and forth under the work light, each scale had been done in painstaking detail and had taken more time than most of her other commissions put together. She had yet to tidy up the edges and polish the piece but already its quality could be seen. Adding the gemstones would be the final touch, making it look perfect. Once finished, the piece will depict a dragon stood on a small mound of gems, each one having been individually chosen by the customer. The finishing piece would be a six millimetre round faceted fire opal that would be clutched within the dragon's claw.

Andromeda's smile widened, so far, this was her best piece and would hopefully bring with it, more commissions and, in turn, improve her life tenfold to what it had been the last year. Since the break up from hell with her ex, her reputation had taken a huge hit. It wasn't beneath Russell to stoop to gossip and slander. She'd had to fight tooth and nail to gain the money to open her shop, and even then commissions were few and far between. The arsehole had truly enjoyed watching as she struggled to live, whilst he lived off the reputation that she had built.

Only she was truly aware of his lack of skill, and it was only after things had gone pear-shaped that Andromeda realised he had been benefitting from her designs. She had thought he was the one; he had done everything to woo her, and then one day, like a bomb exploding around her, she had found out about his lies. At first, she had been crushed, but was willing to possibly give him a second chance, especially when he begged her and told her how much he loved her. That quickly changed when she'd found out he had altered all the names on her designs, gaining credit and royalties behind her back, leaving her almost broke. When she had confronted him, all he had done was laugh and told her she was lucky to have his support as without him, her work would have never been noticed.

The day he had destroyed her life was clear as crystal, there would be no forgetting it. Andromeda could remember every second, every feeling as what she thought was her perfect life crumbled around her.

She had been working late on a joint competition piece that Russell had insisted they do. It was only now that she clearly saw he had left all the work to her. She had walked through her front door, eager to see her man, and hoped he had prepared her some food, only to hear moans and grunts coming from their room. It didn't take a genius to figure out what was going on.

There he was, bare-arsed, going at it more enthusiastically than he had ever done with her, pumping away on top of the same blonde that had been in the shop days earlier to commission that same competition piece.

Her loud, "What the ever-loving fuck," had been met with, "You're home early."

Andromeda had felt like her heart had been pulled from her chest, bounced on the floor like a rubber ball and then stomped on. He had smiled, but never stopped. If she had been a stronger person, she would have knocked him out mid flex. Instead, she had turned and walked out of their home and straight to her best friend's house.

After that, it had taken Russell all of one day to move her out of their home and serve her with documents that stated she'd never actually co-owned the flat. Had he somehow had her name removed? It wouldn't surprise her if he had, Russell had friends in lots of different places and most of them could be bought, he'd proved that when he'd had so much help in spreading rumours about her work, and as such.... Well, here she was. But she would prove that jumped-up cockwomble wrong. Andromeda truly believed in karma – well, that or Barbara getting her way and kneecapping him. She snorted. Barbie threatened that every time someone even remotely upset her, and she loved her friend dearly for it. Russell had ruined her for men; she would either die alone or become a lesbian. At least then she would always know where she stood. There was one issue with that plan: Andromeda liked penis, and she liked men, especially dark-eyed strangers that called to her when she slept. Not that she slept much, and when she did, nine times out of ten she would have nightmares, visions of dying in a multitude of ways; stabbed, poisoned, the list could go on.

Andromeda yawned and looked again at the silver in her hand, sleep was overrated anyway, and that's why they made coffee.

She could sleep when she was dead.

Chapter Three

Aphrodite was bored again, and when she was bored, she usually did one of the following; shopping, although she had run out of room for shoes - who knew they did them in such a wide range of colours and styles; sat in the cute, little coffee shop with that delicious waiter and equally delicious coffee, only she hadn't slept right for weeks after her last splurge – apparently, it had something to do with caffeine; spy and annoy her mortals.

Grinning, she waved her hand, her energies creating her signature seeing pool; a silver stand with twisting vines and roses leading up to a shallow bowl filled with crystal clear water. Waving her hand over the waters, Aphrodite waited as they became clouded before they swirled and revealed her favourite mortal's living room. Arianna was nowhere to be seen, but her male was there.

Sitting comfortably, Aphrodite sipped from her

glass of wine and watched. Her heart told her that today, something important would happen.

"Arianna, Sonia! Are you girls ready yet?"

The deep, husky voice of Arcaeus called out from his sprawled position on the sofa. Craning his head to look over the edge, he shouted again. "Food will be here in a minute."

After glaring the door for a second, he turned back around to look at the TV, the new movie they had bought to watch still paused.

"Why are they getting dressed up to stay in?" Arcaeus grumbled, not expecting an answer but getting one from his best friend regardless of whether he wanted one or not.

"They're women, my friend, no one understands the way they work." Cosmos smirked from his own sprawled position on the other sofa. Cosmos's transition from ancient warrior demigod to personal trainer had been surprisingly quick and easy. He had taken to modern living faster than anyone would have expected. The only hints of his old ways were his speech and his hair, which he kept long. He had become a lot more relaxed than he had been back in ancient Greece, but life in the modern age was a lot easier.

"True, but with them two, I get worried they are up to something." Arcaeus frowned and shot another concerned look towards the bedroom door

"Oh, come on, Arcaeus, stop being so suspicious." Cosmos laughed and turned his attention back to the TV. Arcaeus smiled weakly but continued to fire looks at the bedroom door, they had been in there a good while, but maybe Cosmos was right and he was looking into things too much. His own transition had been a little more difficult, but he put that down to the fact he hadn't been brought to the future but instead been reincarnated. With constant flashbacks from his previous life, at times he found it difficult to differentiate between the then and now. One thing, though, kept him grounded.

Arianna

Even after going through so much herself, she had accepted everything that happened with no question and no complaints. He loved her with every fibre of his being, but lately he felt like there was a wall between them and he was at a complete loss with how to deal with it.

Once again, Arcaeus looked at the door and fought against the need to get up and charge into the room just to find out what was going on. Arianna was his life now and he would avoid, at all costs, anything that would upset her. A deep sigh left him as he faced the TV and made himself concentrate on the screen, the remote in his hand, and not the absence of his love.

Sonia sat on the bed and watched Arianna pace across the width of her bedroom. Her friend's anxious steps worried her. She had noticed something different in her best friend lately. To be honest, they had both changed for the better - who wouldn't when two remarkable men enter your lives and turn your world upside down - but recently, Arianna had become more and more withdrawn and quiet, and not just with Sonia. She had watched her withdraw from Arcaeus as well, and that caused the most concern. Her eyes followed every nervous step, she knew something had been brewing and now she would find out what it was, whether Arianna wanted to reveal it or not.

"Anya," Sonia barked, making Arianna jump, "park ya butt." She smiled and patted the space next to her on the bed.

Arianna looked like she would bolt from the room, but after a few more steps and looking like a deer caught in the headlights, Arianna finally perched next to Sonia on the bed.

Without saying a word, Sonia pulled Arianna's hands onto her lap. Holding them loosely, she closed her eyes and focused. Sonia was still so new to the whole oracle business and usually, she could never bring on a vision. Most of the time they happened randomly and out of her control. But she would try to control it now, if only to help her friend.

"Sonnie, what are you…?"

"Shush, woman." She breathed out. "I'm working."

Sonia peeked out of one eye to see Arianna clamp her mouth shut. She frowned but didn't attempt to talk again.

Squeezing her eyes closed, Sonia focused. She called out to the power she knew she had deep down inside her and pulled on that small butterfly-effect feeling, shaping and willing it to do her bidding. In her mind, she pleaded with her power, willed it to help her until finally, like a piece of a jigsaw, it slotted into place, bringing a flash of light to Sonia's mind that signalled the beginning of a vision.

The trees swayed in the breeze, and with each

dance they released the gold, orange, and brown leaves. The wind collected them, floating them gently to the ground in a symphony of colour. Laughter pulled Sonia's attention and she turned to watch as Arcaeus jogged towards a bench, the very bench Sonia had been sat on when Arianna had confessed to her own strange experience meeting her man. She continued to watch his large form as it bent on one knee in front of …Sonia grinned. Arcaeus was finally doing the right thing and proposing to Arianna.

Her friend looked stunning in the autumn sun, her hair let loose and stirring gently in the wind. Sonia had always been envious of Arianna's natural beauty, but this time it was different; she glowed, her eyes showcased every emotion. Arianna watched Arcaeus with nothing but adoring love, only to change to surprise when he pulled out a ring.

This was the part about being the Oracle she adored, seeing the happiness that the future would bring. She dreaded the bad and prayed she wouldn't get many, not yet anyway.

Sonia smiled more as Arianna enthusiastically nodded her head to Arcaeus's obvious question. Almost ready to pull from the vision, Sonia stopped and gaped. Her gasp was audible as the vision vanished and she was faced once again with the worried expression of her best friend.

Sonia blinked a few times, waiting until Arianna was no longer a blur of skin and hair before she blurted the news right out, unable to hold it in.

"Holy crap, Anya."

Arianna bit her lip and bowed her head, her hands twisting the material of her top. "I know," she replied, her voice quiet.

"What do you mean you know?" Sonia countered. Her answer came as Arianna handed over small white stick.

"Shit a brick, that wasn't the distant future I saw, was it?" she mumbled. Sonia's eyes met those of Arianna once more.

"Well, bugger me, Anya, you're pregnant."

Apollo kicked out at the broken limb of a dried up tree, it had the unfortunate luck of being in his way as he walked the non-descript path through the burning fields of punishment. He had no idea how long he had been trapped in this hell hole; there was nothing to signal the start and finish of the day. The sky was a constant swirl of red and orange as lava from the depths of the earth erupted and spilled onto the plain.

How dare Hades trap him here. He was the sun god, he had rights and duties. Apollo kicked out again, watching as he sent the branch flying into a dark spot. Grunts, squeals, and howls erupted from the disfigured and monstrous souls that hid there. They were here because of their crimes, yet Apollo had done nothing wrong. He may have tortured and killed Arcaeus, but look how that had turned out.

Even his own son had treated him poorly. What had he done to deserve that?

But most of all, it was Hades to whom he focussed his ire. Although he was one of the elder gods, he had no right to treat Apollo as he did.

He had no doubts he would get out of his current entrapment, but he had to do it without his fellow gods knowing. The only one he could trust was Persephone, but she had been surprisingly quiet lately. Although trapped, the fools had still left him with some of his powers, and he took full advantage of them now as he waved his hand, creating a stunning gold bowl that stood on an intricate stand. Stepping close, he looked into the waters and called out, "Persephone."

The bowl erupted in a bright light before it dulled

and showed the stunningly beautiful goddess lounged completely naked.

"Having fun, I see, goddess," Apollo grated out. Yes, she was beautiful, but there was something in her eyes that hadn't been there when he had first decided to have fun with her. He had shown her his perverted loves and she had thrown herself into them with gusto. He may have created a monster, but it would be a monster to further his own gain.

"Apollo, darling, how are the fields of punishment?" she asked jovially, and leaned towards her own pool to look closer. "You don't look happy," she said, stating the obvious, and Apollo rolled his eyes in annoyance.

"Why would I be happy here? I swear you are frustratingly stupid, Persephone."

The insult made the goddess flinch, and he watched as her chocolate brown eyes hardened.

"Is there a reason for this call or did you just want to insult me more? I do have things to do, you know, besides talk to you." Her voice was sing-song in its sound, but there was something that rose the hairs on the back of his neck.

"Persephone, you are to help me get free of this place."

"You want me to help you get free?" she asked, a smile playing across her ruby red lips.

"Yes, fucking understatement of the year that is, goddess. So, what are you doing to help my situation?" He almost shouted into the bowl, his frustration getting the better of him.

"Help?" she purred, and sat back on her lounger. At one time, Apollo would have grown hard just from the sight of her luscious naked form, but now he found it lacking. That might have been his fault.

"Why should I help you?" she asked quietly. "You have promised me a lot of things, Apollo, and have never delivered."

She stood, and Apollo could do nothing but wait as she opened her arms, letting her servants clothe her in a dress of stunning gold. His own colour. Apollo's right eye twitched. He could feel the anger as it oiled up inside him. She had taken him for a fool.

Faking a smile, he answered, "Goddess, have you forgotten our time together? Forgive me, I am just frustrated at being trapped here, and seeing you look so beautiful… It makes me wish I were there."

The lie flew easily from his lips, and he watched her face as she became lost in the memories of their time together; multiple sexual encounters that introduced her to the darker side of love-making. But it wasn't love, was it? It was merely fucking. That's where he had screwed up.

Yes, he had promised her a great many things, and had done an even greater many things to her. She was now no longer the innocent goddess her mother thought her to be, and she wasn't exactly the same sane goddess either. Apollo had to admit that somewhere amongst their meetings, the goddess had lost a lot more than simple innocence.

"Goddess, help me get out of here and I will finally give you what you want."

Her eyes lightened and she smiled. "What I want…"

Apollo nodded. She had always wanted to be his queen, to be by his side as he tried to take over Olympus.

"Yes, my dear, be by my side forever," he cooed.

Persephone sat once again on her cushioned chair, her dark hair falling around her. Her gaze almost searing through him, she answered with a chilling smile. "What I want has changed, Apollo, and I'm afraid you are no longer a part of the deal."

"What!" he shouted.

"Hush now, I may still have need of you, so be a good sun god and stay put, that way I can keep an eye on you."

Apollo was stunned, his only hope of freedom was conspiring against him, using everything he had taught her. He was being beaten by a goddess.

"I know, I know, hard to believe that little ole me has gotten the better of you, but believe it or not, I'm a quick learner." She laughed to herself. "You already knew that, though, didn't you?"

Stunned into silence, he watched the pool, almost afraid of what he may hear.

"I will be the one that takes Olympus," she said simply. "So, I would appreciate it if you wouldn't… fuck it up." She almost salivated on the mortal word.

Apollo said nothing as the seeing pool flashed again and the image of Persephone vanished, only the chilling smile she had on her face remained seared in his mind.

Purgatory now seemed a better place to be, here he wouldn't be disturbed, here he could plan.

Seating himself on a rock, Apollo waved his hand and watched as another basin appeared, the liquid reflecting his own image back at him. Closing his eyes, Apollo focused all the power he had left. Swirls of gold and silver surrounded him before they flowed into the basin. He opened his eyes and watched as scene after scene flickered across the surface before it finally settled on the concerned face of a mortal male.

It had been the same male he had managed to influence earlier, before he had spoken to Persephone. It was then he realised that he was completely out of power.

Looking into the mortal's green eyes, he grinned as they changed to his own gold.

"Don't worry, Clint, I will take it from here."

Apollo had a plan to get his power back, and to get revenge on those that thought they could lock him away. He had felt the presence on an old power that had been released upon the mortal realm, and that would be his ticket out of this literal hellhole. He would go after the Essence, and then the gods of Olympus.

Chapter Four

Andromeda let out a breath as her last collection left her shop. She watched as her client almost bounced into the waiting taxi, his new purchase in hand. The dragon pendant had beaten all expectations, and now her reputation was on its way back up. The client had taken one look and grinned from ear to ear. He had even given her a hug, which had taken them both by surprise.

The piece wasn't the easiest she had ever made. In total, it had taken about 48 hours to craft, but it had been worth it. This was why she had chosen to be a silversmith; working with the metal and creating something unique and spectacular out of it calmed her soul in a way nothing else ever did.

For years she had felt like she was always the one on the outside, the one that wanted in on the action but didn't know how to do it. Even with Russell, she had always been the one on the outskirts of the room whist he did all the mingling. She didn't have many friends; she had been the one that was easiest to forget. Her mother had been the one person that Andromeda could count on, her and Barbie. But Barbie was more like a sister than a friend. Andromeda loved her mother with all her heart, but she could only stand a few hours around her.

Her mother was a born-again hippy and had taken to living in a caravan park on the outskirts of the city. She had everything she needed and made her money by making hand-dyed clothes, beaded jewellery, and reading tarot cards.

Andromeda waited as the shutters on the shop front slowly closed. Others walked past on their way home, some stopping to wave, and she couldn't help but let a full smile loose. The money she had received for the pendant would not only pay all the bills this month but also give her some extra. The more commissions she did the more her reputation as a master silversmith would grow again.

She knew Russell wouldn't be able to hold up the pretence of being the one that did the work, and she would be there smiling when it bit him on the arse.

Andromeda quietly walked through her shop, making sure all the lights were off before she locked the back door. Throwing all the bolts in place, she then turned to the small door hidden near the back of the shop. She had chosen this property to rent not because it was cheap but because it came with a flat.

At the top of the stairs, it opened into a simple studio apartment. The bedroom area was to the right, her queen-sized bed in the corner with only a fabric wardrobe and a tiny table that held a mirror. This was separated from the rest of the room by simple screens. On the left was the kitchen that just managed to hold a dining table, and a tiny lounge that held a sofa and TV directly in front of it. The only other door was to her minute bathroom. Yes, it was small, but it was hers.

After being in such a large flat with Russell, she found she enjoyed the compact space more, and she enjoyed being on her own in it. He had been controlling, not allowing her to make the place hers, not letting her unpack any of her things. Maybe she should have realised then, but she had thought herself in love.

Near the TV stood her desk and chair, this was where she drew her designs and would sometimes spend all night bringing her ideas to life. Only lately, the only thing she had drawn were a pair of intense dark eyes. From a distance they appeared black, but on closer inspection they were blue, a royal blue that shimmered with emotion. She could never see the entire face, it was only ever the eyes, and the dark husky voice that would forever remain with her.

Kicking her shoes off, Andromeda headed to the bathroom. She would have a hot shower, grab one of those easy microwavable meals and sit in front of the TV until she fell asleep. Deliberately leaving her things spread about in a silent rebellion towards her ex, she grinned. He had more OCD problems than anyone she had ever know. She had spent evening after evening cleaning and keeping everything in its right place, all because it made him twitch.

If she thought about it more, she would say it wasn't OCD, he was just a twat. He may have hurt her, tried to break her, even damaged her heart, but she was happy she was free, even if she hadn't realised it at the time.

Her home phone's loud, shrilling ring brought Andromeda out of her musings and into the kitchen.

"Hello," she answered, not sure who would want to call her at half seven at night.

"Andromeda, baby."

"Mum," she replied in relief. "Are you ok?" she asked. Her mother never called her in the week, only on a Sunday morning before she was due to open her tarot shop.

"Yes, darling, I'm fine. I'm calling to check on you, my cards had a strange reading today." Her mother sounded concerned, but she would rely on the card readings more than anything else. It could be pissing down with rain and in full view yet because the cards said it would be sunny, that's what she believed.

"I'm fine, Mum, nothing has happened."

"Mmmm," she heard over the phone.

"Mum, are you ok?" Andromeda could only hear shuffling as her mother played with her cards.

"Mum," she called again.

"Oh, hi, Andromeda, fancy you calling me."

Andromeda sighed and sat at her small table, this was one of the reasons she had moved away from her mother. She had the memory of a fish. It was only because she had so much else going on in her life that she forgot the small things.

"Andromeda, I must go, thank you for calling your old mum, but your namesake is on the TV and you know I can't miss it. Love you, little girl."

"Love you, Mum." Andromeda had barely answered when the click sounded, signalling her mother had put the phone down.

Yes, she loved that woman, but only in small doses, her eccentricity was too much to handle at times. For example, what woman names her child not after the famed Aethiopian Princess of Greek mythology but in fact the SyFy TV show? She had also gained the same nickname and was called Rommie on a regular basis, mostly by her best friend, Barbara. She didn't mind that as much as having to explain why she had such an unusual name.

Placing the phone back into its cradle, Andromeda pulled a small bottle of beer from the fridge, collected her dated mobile phone, and headed to the bathroom. A shower just wouldn't cut it, she would spend her evening floating in the tub and texting her friend. Tomorrow was Saturday and she had decided she was well overdue a night out.

Aphrodite didn't bother to change back into her goddess attire for her meeting with Hades. She found she preferred the comfort of the jeans she wore and the softness of the woollen turtleneck jumper she had purchased, as recommended by Sonia. She strutted into his temple, her heeled boots clacking on the marble floor.

"You called, Hades," she shouted. She had been waiting on his summons. Her own heart had felt his need back when she had nearly died, and if they didn't do something about it the whole of the underworld would be in peril.

"Hades," she asked again and continued through the temple. Why call her and then not be around to receive her? As she made her way through the rooms of the temple, she was astounded by its simple beauty. Instead of gold everywhere, like in most of the gods homes, this one was simply white marble and black onyx. The contrast was breathtaking. The ceilings were all painted like the night sky and twinkled with gemstones that showcased each and every constellation. So absorbed she was in the spectacle that was Hades' home she almost missed the voices that echoed from Hades' private chamber.

"Oh, come, Hades." Asoft, feminine voice could be heard. "I am sorry for how I treated you before, let's make up and be friends."

Aphrodite frowned as she recognised the voice. She tilted her head as she walked on, peeking around the corner to see a very tense Hades, his chest being stroked by Persephone.

"Goddess, please don't touch me," he growled out, and took a step away.

Not to be deterred, Persephone moved forward

again. "Oh, don't be like that. We can be friends, can't we?"

"No," Hades stated. "No, we can't. After all, Persephone, I am just a monster, a monster that rules the dead. Who could be friends with such a cold-hearted man?"

Aphrodite smiled as Hades fired back at the goddess with her own hurtful words from years before. Demeter had wanted a union between the two and at the time, Hades had been willing to try, thinking there was no other option for him. Instead, Persephone had sneered and shown open disgust at the idea, and in front of the whole pantheon, turned Hades down.

"Oh pish, I was young and stupid," she countered, and Aphrodite watched as Hades tensed. As much as Hades was a grumpy, moody god, he had his reasons, and as love, it was her job to help him find his soulmate. If that meant prying a goddess's claws out of him, then she would. She had been bored, maybe messing with this goddess was what she needed.

Stepping out from her hiding place, she made her entrance loud.

"Hades, honey, you called me?" She strutted

towards the two, answering Persephone's glare with a bubbly smile.

"Persephone, darling, how are you doing? It's been a while." Aphrodite kissed the goddess on both cheeks, stealthily moving herself so she was between the two.

"Goddess," Persephone answered, almost sulkily. "What does love need with death?" she asked outright.

Aphrodite smiled again, ignoring the hardness in Persephone's words, and the outright nosiness.

"It's Friday," she answered simply. "Movie night."

"Movie night?" the goddess answered, looking confused.

"Yes, movie night. Myself and Hades head over to the mortal realm and enjoy the delights of popcorn and movies." The lie easily fell from Aphrodite's lips, but she refused to inform anyone of the real reason she was there. She had made a promise to Hades; to help him and keep it from all of Olympus. If Persephone happened to get the complete wrong idea about her visit, then so be it.

"Yes, movie night," Hades agreed, although she knew he had no clue what she was referring to.

"Fine, I was just leaving anyway. Hades, honey, think on what I've said." Persephone smiled sweetly and blew a kiss before turning on her heel and heading for the exit, her dress billowing out behind her, showing off her clearly naked form underneath.

"Ack, I'm going to need mind bleach to get rid of that little show and tell."

"What's mind bleach?" Hades' innocent question made her laugh, this god had a lot to learn, and he would need to learn it quickly if he stood any chance of finding his soulmate before her fated time to descend into Elyssia.

"We will cover that later. Come, let's discuss the plan and how we should proceed." The god nodded and turned, only to stop.

"I don't want her, Aphrodite, I never have. I just thought I had no option, but now…" He stopped and their gazes met. "I know I do, and I would give up my immortality if it meant I could spend a single lifetime with my soulmate." His words were quiet but they hit Aphrodite in the heart and the gut. Her own gift flared and gave her hope that the god would get his wish, even if she had to beg, borrow and steal from the cosmos itself to make it happen.

Aphrodite nodded. "Let's get started then."

Chapter Five

Curled up in the arms of Arcaeus, Arianna felt content - and irritable. After her one-on-one with Sonia and the truth about her current condition coming out, she was more nervous than before. She had to tell Arcaeus, but she was scared.

They had technically only been together a few months, six if you add in the time she spent back in ancient Greece. But still, was that enough time to say, *Hey, honey, I know we've only been together a short time and we still have so much to learn about each other, but guess what…I'm up the duff.*

Arianna rolled her eyes. In her head, she sounded like a complete and utter dipstick. She knew he loved her, that was never in question - the love they shared had proved it transcended time - but what she didn't know was is if he wanted children. Some men didn't.

How do you bring that up in a conversation when

you've never actually discussed it before? She closed her eyes and settled fully into his embrace, hoping sleep may bring some answers, but she wasn't holding her breath.

"Mortals!" a deep, booming voice called from her hallway, causing Arianna to scream. Arcaeus reacted as any warrior would; pushing her behind him and facing the unknown foe with only his bare hands as weapons.

"Fuck, where did I put my sword?" Arianna heard him shout from her new position on the floor - on her arse.

She couldn't help it, she started to giggle, and the giggles got worse as the owner of the voice walked into the lounge, a proud smile upon his face.

"Hades," Arcaeus grated out, obviously annoyed at the intrusion. "To what do we owe this pleasure?"

Arianna continued to giggle as she moved off her arse and to her knees before crawling onto the sofa. Leaning across the back, she admired the god. She'd always had a soft spot for him, and without admitting it out loud, he was the best-looking of all the gods - in that dark, brooding sort of way. Only, he wasn't brooding now. His grin lit up his face and made the god even more gorgeous.

"Mortals," he started, and walked fully into the

room, sinking down onto the plush seat of the other sofa. His toga-clad body wiggled a little to get comfy and then he turned his gaze back to them.

"Where are the other two, the Oracle and Son of Apollo?" he asked, sounding a little disappointed.

"Please, make yourself at home," Arcaeus growled out sarcastically as he stood and folded his arms across his chest.

"Thank you, I will," Hades replied, the sarcasm going over his head completely.

Arianna snorted unladylike and turned once again on the sofa, seating herself properly on the cushions. Reaching up, she tugged on Arcaeus's t-shirt, bidding him to sit down.

"Sit, honey, please."

Never taking his eyes from Hades he unfolded his arms, reached down and took her hand, before sitting on the edge of the sofa next to her.

"So, Lord Hades, to what do we owe this pleasure," Arianna asked, actually quite keen to know what had brought the God of the underworld from his domain and to her home. The only immortal to ever seek her out was, of course, Aphrodite, who had quickly become a dear friend and regularly sought herself and Sonia out for a little bit of girl time.

Arianna watched the god as he ignored her question and looked about her apartment, his eyes taking in every aspect as if he had never seen these things before. The TV caught his attention, and he even leaned forward to take in the movie that was on.

"Hades," Arcaeus bit out.

"Ah yes, Aphrodite sent me," he started, then paused, seemingly embarrassed all of a sudden. "She informed me that if I wanted help in fitting in amongst the mortals then I would need the advice of a mortal," he stopped again, waving his arms at himself, "and here I am."

Silence filled the room as Arcaeus took the remote control from the table and turned the TV off, then sat back on the sofa, his arms automatically reaching around Arianna and pulling her close. Arianna had gotten used to him doing that whenever another male was in the room. Part of her loved it, loved his open possession of her. Another part made her want to tell him to get a grip.

"Why should we help you?" Arcaeus asked.

"Arcaeus!" Arianna chastised.

"What?" he asked, and looked down at her, his eyes hard. "Why should we help the gods, what do they ever do for us besides bring disaster? Look what we've had to go through because of them."

Arianna frowned and argued back, "You forget,

my love, that if it wasn't for the gods, we would never have what we have now. I would have never gone back to you."

He was about to argue again but Arianna was fed up with his mood swings and grumps, especially when it came to discussing the gods.

"If you are not happy with what happened, that's fine. We can't change the past, you know this," Arianna snapped, then turned to Hades. "What can we do to help you?"

Hades watched the two mortals carefully, they seemed very tense with each other. But the hostility from the warrior made Hades pause for thought.

Was that how most mortals felt about the interference of the gods, did they all hate them as much as Arcaeus? He had been away from the mortal world for a very long time and had forgotten what it was like to converse with them, to ask them for something and not demand. All the gods and goddesses on Olympus were guilty of this, they had been spoiled for far too long. Hades agreed with Aphrodite, it was time they got off their immortal arses and started to enjoy the world once again.

Hades was determined to change, change his ways and what people actually thought of him. It would start with these mortals that meant so much to the goddess of love. She had threatened him when she had suggested he come to them for help. Her words had stopped him in his tracks and it had taken a while for it to sink in as to what she meant. She'd implied, simply don't hurt them or she would make sure he never had his soulmate. As love herself, he believed her threat like no others.

Coughing into his fist, he brought both sets of eyes his way, the tension in the room, for once, making him uncomfortable.

"Mortals, please do not argue," he started, and only received a glare from the male. "Aphrodite said you would help me with the small things, like clothing and…" He stopped again. How did a god ask for help in courting a female? He knew his current demanding ways would not work, and he really did need all the help he could get.

"I need… err… help with… ermm… speaking to a female," he rushed out, and then sat and waited. He wasn't sure what he expected, but the deep laughter from the warrior was not it.

"You are kidding, right?"

"Arcaeus, don't be so rude." Arianna elbowed the male.

"What? It is a little funny, the elder god of Olympus wants advice on women. This is definitely something you don't get to hear every day."

"You are being an arse, Arcaeus," Arianna snapped.

Arcaeus looked down at the female and his gaze dropped as she continued to glare at him, her anger palpable even from where Hades sat.

"I'll call Cosmos and Sonia," he replied quietly, and stood. Taking a small metal object from his pocket, Hades watched, amazed when he pressed something on it and then held it to his head, speaking into the item.

"Why do you need our help with this, Hades? As he said," she tilted her head at Arcaeus, "you are an elder god, surely you don't have issues with getting a woman."

Again, Hades was taken aback by what people actually thought of him and about his reputation. He was nothing like his brother Zeus, who was a known womaniser. But she was right in the sense most gods didn't have to try very hard to get any female into bed.

Hades made the decision to be as honest as possible, even at the risk of looking weak.

"I need your help because I want what you have," he stated simply. "I want my soulmate. I want her love and I want it forever."

Arianna's eyes widened and Arcaeus stopped smirking and sat back down.

"You know who she is?" the warrior asked, his face now serious.

Hades nodded. "I know roughly where she is, but that is all. I have known about her for hundreds of years yet I have never been able to find her. Each time I see her it is in the underworld and she has died. Each incarnation is different, and I am always too late."

"Oh, my..." Arianna replied quietly, and he saw the genuine sadness in her eyes.

"I want the soul-encompassing love that you two share, and I would give up anything to have it."

Hades' heart hurt when he thought of the many times he had missed out on seeing his soulmate before she had perished, all those times he hadn't managed to save her. He wanted one chance to get to know her, to show her the love he had for her, and that he would, if she demanded, change even the heavens themselves for her. His eyes followed Arcaeus as the warrior stood and walked the short distance to him. Holding out a large hand, Arcaeus waited until Hades took it.

"Whatever you need help with, you will have it." Arcaeus looked back at Arianna and smiled. "No one should miss out on a chance at love, not even the god of the dead."

Chapter Six

"Rommie," Barbara called from across the bar. Andromeda looked up as she was bent over the pool table about to play her shot. "It's your round."

Andromeda took her time in lining up the cue, and then fired, shooting a ball into a pocket before she stood and placed the cue against the wall.

"Babs, we both know you're talking crap, it's your round." She grinned. "That's why you're at the bar, after all."

She watched as her ginger-haired, four-feet-nine pixie of a friend casually threw her the middle finger and then finally ordered two beers.

Barbara - or Barbie, as Andromeda had always called her - was named as such because she was almost a living incarnation of the doll. Super skinny, huge boobs, and large blue eyes that could look as innocent as a babe. The only physical difference was her carrot-topped head. It also didn't help that she had a mouth on her that would rival most sailors. Every other word was usually foul, but she was her best friend and there was nothing she would change.

She was the loud to Andromeda's quiet, as well as the tart in their friendship. Barbie wasn't afraid of doing anything, never mind chatting up guys. After the breakup that had taken almost everything from her, she had lost friends that were not, in fact, friends at all. They had been the hangers on, ones that latched onto the successful in the hopes of gaining some themselves. They had believed every scrap of bullshit that had been vomited from Russell's mouth and hadn't found it difficult to set her loose and forget about her. So lost in the memory of that time, it took more than a moment to register the bottle of beer being waved in front of her face.

"Yo, Earth to Rommie, come in."

"Huh?" was all Andromeda could come out with as the bottle was thrust into her hand. Barbie laughed.

"Where's the glass?" Andromeda asked as she looked at the bottle then back at her friend.

Barbara shrugged. "The cutie at the bar mentioned something about ladies using glasses, but I assumed he was talking about someone else 'cause we ain't ladies." She grinned before swigging from the bottle and then wiped her mouth with the back of her hand, emphasising the fact she wasn't much of a lady.

Andromeda raised an eyebrow and looked passed her best friend to the barman who was wiping glasses. He was cute, in a young surfer-look sort of way. His green eyes stood out from his boyish face, and when he met her gaze, he smiled, showing off dimples that would have most girls going all gooey-eyed. His smile soon fell as his gaze moved to Barbie, and his whole demeanour went to looking almost frightened as he vanished into the back room of the bar.

With a frown, Andromeda turned and faced her friend who was currently perched over the pool table, a thigh thrown over the corner, in an attempt to get in line to take a shot. Barbie definitely dealt with short girl issues.

"Barbie… What did you do?"

Barbara continued fighting her way onto the pool table, taking her time before striking the cue ball and firing a striped one towards the pocket. Luckily for Andromeda, she missed completely.

"Barbie," she called out again.

"What?" she called back as she jumped from her perch. She attempted to look innocent, but Andromeda had known her far too long.

"What did you do?" she repeated.

Barbara took her time as she picked up her bottle and almost drained the contents. Her eyebrow lifted as she looked at Andromeda. The look one of pure guilt.

"What the hell did you do this time?"

Still no answer. Andromeda growled. "Barbie."

Andromeda folded her arms and waited for Barbie to quit stalling. She took her time, sipping her drink, then placed the empty bottle on the table nearby before looking Andromeda in the eye.

"Fine," she huffed, finally realising Andromeda wasn't about to let it go. "Lamb chop, behind the bar," she grinned, "asked me if I wanted to 'hang out'.

Andromeda sat down, it was better if she was already in a chair as Barbie had a tendency to shock the crap out of her - and she always wished she was sat when she found out. A part of her hoped that this wasn't as bad as the last time.

"And? I'm assuming you said no as you seem to avoid any bloke that seems normal." Andromeda expected the middle finger that flew up once again, but she was right. Barbara didn't date normal men, she dated strange men that did strange shit, like getting themselves arrested for indecent exposure whilst trying to sexually assault their own motorbike. Nope, Barbie didn't do normal.

"You would be correct, Rommie, in me saying no. He is, as you have so loudly put it, too normal," she hissed out, "He is far too innocent for my tastes. I would corrupt him and, of course, ruin him for all women, and that would be selfish of me."

Andromeda rolled her eyes, tooting her own horn was another of Barbie's talents. "So, what's the issue then?"

"Bless his little cotton socks, he was a little too keen - annoyingly keen - and didn't take my initial no for an answer. He then asked, 'why not'."

"Oh…" Andromeda groaned, that never went well. Barbie and honesty was never a good combination and had, on occasion, got them kicked out of clubs before.

"What did you say?" Andromeda asked, not sure she actually wanted to hear the answer.

"I kept it simple. I just said my vagina was tired."

Andromeda blinked. "That was it?" she asked. That was on the tame side for Barbie.

"Yeah, but bless him, he just wouldn't leave it. He then asked if was available after my vagina had rested. Kind of sweet, in a way."

"Right, sweet… Yeah, that's what it was." Andromeda wanted to bang her head on the nearby table. "So, if you found him sweet, but told him no, why is he looking over here like he's ready to bolt?"

"Oh, yeah..." Barbie started, "I may have said - after he wouldn't leave it - that I wasn't ready to share my herpes status with him yet, but if he was serious, then we would have to go *really* slow."

Andromeda said nothing, only stared at her friend. What the hell do you say to that? Keeping silent, Andromeda picked up her bottle and took a long swig, her mind swirling with a continuous repeat of 'what he fuck?'. Barbara never failed to surprise her, or worry her about getting arrested.

"Your shot, Rommie, so shift ya fat arse."

Firing back her own middle finger, Andromeda stood and once again looked towards the bar. The young man was still there, and she had to admire the fact he hadn't yet bolted. She sent him an apologetic smile, but it was too little too late. Barbie had scarred another one.

Picking up her cue, Andromeda approached the pool table. After choosing her ball, she bent over and aimed. Her concentration was screwed, so she wasn't surprised when the ball hit the corner of the pocket and bounced off.

"Typical," she mumbled, and moved her braid back over her shoulder. "Barbie, your shot, and, for once, stop scaring the staff. I actually like it in here and would prefer not to have to find yet another pub to be our local."

"You worry too much," Barbie countered as she picked up her own cue and walked around the table. "You need to lighten up." She grinned, then came to a stop. "Speaking of which, when are you planning on 'getting back on the horse'?" she asked, her fingers doing air quotes. "'Bout time, don't you think?"

"No," Andromeda answered, but didn't elaborate.

"Err… yes. Your hoohah must be all dried up by now. You don't want it to go out of action completely."

"Barbie!"

"What?" she answered as she bent over the table and proceeded to pot her balls, winning the game.

"I am not getting back on the horse - or whatever you want to describe it as. I've had enough of that bullshit."

Andromeda stood and walked around the table, hoping that re-racking the balls would end the conversation, but she should have known better; with Barbie, that wasn't going to happen. She didn't need her day off turning into a therapy session.

"Listen, Rommie, let's forget about horses and

maybe focus on the fact you are - and don't you dare shout at me – lonely."

"I am not; I am perfectly happy," Andromeda countered.

"Bullshit," Barbara called out as she laid her cue down and walked around the table until she was stood in front of Andromeda. Her face serious for once.

"You can't bury yourself in work, Rommie. You can't use it to hide away from the world and the prospect of loving again."

Andromeda couldn't look her friend in the eye; she was right, after all. But she was scared to take that step. She was still young, but the whole idea of letting someone in, giving someone the chance to hurt her just the same as Russell had… She honestly didn't know if her heart could take it.

"Rommie, look at me."

She forced herself to look into her best friend's eyes, where she saw only love and support.

"I want you happy, and because of that douche, you haven't been for a while." Barbara smiled and placed her arm around Andromeda's shoulders. "So, I have a cunning plan to help things," she wiggled her fingers, "motor along."

Andromeda groaned. "No! not one of you plans. I already told you, I don't want to get arrested."

Barbara just grinned in response. "Don't fret, this one is tame and there is no backing out."

She groaned again, her insides somersaulting as she dreaded what was to come. She could just walk out, but Barbie's challenges always got her competitive side going.

"Fine, name it." She smiled back, determined to see the fun side and not dwell on the negatives.

Barbie whooped and turned Andromeda to face the entrance of the pub, her hands on her shoulders squeezing a little.

"Your challenge, Rommie," she whispered. "Do a Grease 2."

Andromeda's mind whirled. What was a Grease 2? It must be something that happened in the film, but she hadn't seen it in years. Then a single spark stuck. She knew what she had to do.

"A Grease 2?" she questioned as she swallowed. This was not going to end well.

"Yep," Barbie answered, and to confirm what she thought, Barbie gave out the details, "You have to kiss the next guy that walks through the door."

"Ahh shit, I hate you, Barbie."

"Nah, you don't, you fucking adore me."

Andromeda squealed as Barbie smacked her on the arse. "Now, go get em, tiger."

Andromeda groaned but moved forward. Maybe she should have stayed in bed today. That would have been a better idea

Yes, staying in bed would have been a much better idea.

Hades stood and looked up at the sign that hung over the entrance of the mortal establishment he was about to enter. Aphrodite, in her godessly wisdom, had informed him to arrive and enter the building by a certain time if he wanted to see his soulmate. Then the mortals had given him advice on what to wear and what to say. Although, some of the things they'd said had confused the hell out of him.

At least Arianna and Sonia had been honest, they had even called him a little chauvinistic when he had assumed courting his woman would be easy. That had not settled well in his gut, and the prospect of a difficult courting was oozing dread into his mind. Still, here he was, dressed in what was described by Sonia as a 'drool-worthy outfit'. All in black, he wore jeans that rested on his hips but seemed to cup his buttocks well. He liked the feel of the material, although it did chafe just a little on his bollocks, but he had agreed with Cosmos on not wearing the modern underwear - he didn't want them strangled. His t-shirt, as the girls had called it, stretched tightly over his chest and arms. They seemed to think this would help his case. Whatever they thought would work, he would go with, they were, after all, more informed than him.

So, here he stood, outside The Golden Goat, his first ever venture into a pub. This was where mortals went to congregate and drink, as well as meet potential mates. The outside wasn't that impressive, it only had the one sign showing what it was called, and a tiny doorway. Shaking his head, he pushed the wooden door and ducked to stop his skull from hitting the lintel. Why mortals made things this small, he didn't know. Surely there were others his size. The smell of beer and something else he was unable to identify greeted him as he stepped inside.

The interior was dark, with lamps dotted here and there, along with larger lamps that were above tables that had balls on them. The atmosphere was cosy and intimate, a huge contrast to the initial feeling of dull and depressing. He liked it instantly, it reminded him of the taverns of his youth, when he used to venture to the mortal world. A place where he could hide from the drama of Olympus and sit in comfort. Hades smiled, he would most definitely come back here after his courting was done, maybe his mate would come with him and they could 'date'. He tilted his head, that was the word Arianna had used, wasn't it?

Hades' inner ramblings were quickly supressed as he eyed a female walking in his direction. She was smaller than his huge frame, almost nymph-like in the way she moved. Her hair was pulled back into a long braid that hung over her shoulder, its colour he could only compare to that of the whitest alabaster produced by the earth herself. It shimmered under the dull lights - an unusual colour, but one that stood out with its beauty. Her eyes called to him, a cerulean blue, and were framed by dark lashes, a contrast to the hair on her head. She was still moving towards him, maybe she wanted to leave. That thought alone made his gut tighten.

The closer she got to him, the quicker his heartrate sped up. His palms became sweaty and his mouth dry.

What was happening to him?

The female stopped in front of him, her eyes widening as she assessed the length of his form. He was well aware of his attributes, and if he so desired he could have many females, but he didn't. He wanted one; the one made for him and him alone.

Still, this female, who barely reached his chest, had caught his attention. It wasn't just her beauty or her form, but, in fact, it was the depth of emotion in her eyes, a knowledge and ageless soul that was buried there. It called to him, to his immortality, to his very soul.

Was this her?

Could she be his?

Unaware of the turmoil going through the female's head, he was stunned as she pulled on his t-shirt until he was bent over slightly. Then, placing a palm across the back of his neck, she pulled him forward before - in an unexpected move - she placed her lips against his.

Her taste as she explored his lips was unlike anything he had tasted before, it exploded his taste buds, igniting a need he hadn't felt for years. She was sweeter than the elderberries that graced the Elyssian fields and more addictive than ambrosia itself. He opened, allowing her all the access she wanted. He would let her take control for this first kiss - it would be the first of many. With a groan, his hands found her waist and he pulled her closer, only to have her own hands stop his as she pushed against his chest and broke away from the kiss. Her lips were swollen and her eyes glazed, but they held a confusion that he, too, had felt at the start, but he understood fully now.

She was his soulmate. This was the woman he had come to find. Still, he said nothing and let her pull away.

"Thanks for playing along," she said, her voice a velvet whisper to his ears as she smiled shyly up at him. "You sure can kiss," she breathed out, and Hades watched as a blush travelled up her neck and onto her cheeks. He felt almost smug that he had done that.

"See you around, big guy," she said, her eyes holding his captive as she walked passed him and towards another female who stood waiting. They exchanged words, but Hades was unable to make out what was being said before they moved out of sight. His only consolation was the fact the female had kept looking at him, her eyes constantly moving over his from as if she was trying to commit it to memory.

"Wow, you lucky bastard."

The voice came from a male who was stood behind the bar, and it pulled his attention away from his female. Fighting every instinct he had to follow her, pick her up, and take her to his realm where they would continue the kiss, he walked to the bar before sitting on one of the high stools.

"Lucky how?" he asked. Aphrodite had told him to take it slow, to not pursue like he would have in ancient times. So, he would learn as much as he could about this mortal art of wooing.

And then…

Then she wouldn't stand a chance.

Chapter Seven

The water looked crystal clear, the depths only a slightly darker shade of turquoise than the surface. Hints of blues and even golds swirled as the current swept passed. The waters called to her, enticed her to drink her fill and forget, to think no more of the pain of her past life, the agony of missing loved ones. To drink and all would be well.

Their voices filled her head, coaxing in a loving song that few could deny. This was the River Lethe, the river of rebirth and forgetting.

Her heart had been torn, the pain unbearable as she had made her way through the paths of the underworld. She missed her family, as was expected, but she also missed her love. Childbirth had taken her before she had even the pleasure of hearing her child cry, seeing its perfect face, finding out whether she had been graced with a boy or a girl. That pain hurt the most.

"My lady," a deep voice called, pulling her thoughts away from her life and what she missed. Turning her head, she watched as the lord and god of the underworld approached. She had heard rumours of his magnificence, only they didn't do him justice. He was tall, a man built of pure muscle and perfection, as the gods should be. But what caught her attention were his eyes. Royal blue, almost black, they held a pain in their depths that called to her.

"Are you ok?" he asked simply. Nearly forgetting herself, she bowed quickly, tearing her eyes away from his own.

"My Lord." Keeping her head bowed, she answered honestly, "I am merely deciding whether I will choose to be reborn or not."

"Ahh, I see. Have you decided?" he asked, his voice sending goose bumps across her skin.

"I want to, my lord, but I fear forgetting my past or who I am."

"Then why don't you stay?" he said simply, but the emotion in his words had her looking up into a face far too beautiful for its own good.

"Stay? Stay in the underworld?" she asked.

He simply nodded, and she felt an intense wave of déjà vu, like she had been in this exact spot and had heard him say the exact same thing. She knew what her answer would be, just the same as she knew what his reaction would be. What it had always been.

"How many times have I visited this river?" she asked. Her heart knew it had been many, and the pain that once again flickered across his face, along with his next words, told her that this was not her first visit.

"Too many to count or remember." His voice, deep and quiet, pulled at her soul. He stepped closer and took her ghostly hand, her own skin pale and luminescent in comparison to his. She watched as the ruler of the underworld bent over and kissed her hand, and even dead, she felt the shivers that travelled through her from his touch.

"I pray you live a good life and we not meet again for a long time. For we will meet again; death is always certain." Hades paused as he released her hand.

"Fear not, my lady, you will always remember who you are as long as you stay true to your soul," he said, then turned, his form quickly vanishing amongst the trees of the underworld.

Those eyes would remain with her, of that she had no doubt.

Those eyes called to her soul.

Andromeda awakened slowly to see the ceiling of her apartment. She could see the flecks of paint that needed a touch up and the cracks that needed filling, but amongst all that, she could see the royal blue orbs of the stranger from her dreams. The dreams were becoming more frequent, each a different time but always the same scenario. Either she was dying, or she was dead and at a river. The last time she had researched her dreams, much to the delight of her mother, she had only found references to ancient Greek myths of a river that allowed you to be reborn. So, would that make the stranger Hades? Only, he was no longer just a dream, he was the man she had accosted and snogged on a dare in the pub the night before. Their eyes were identical, but they dressed completely different. It did make her wonder if she was slowly losing her mind from the lack of male contact.

But that man…

What a specimen he had been, dressed all in black - which he pulled off - with muscles upon muscles. He could have easily flexed his way out of that tight t-shirt, and she wouldn't have minded one bit. Nope, she would have been cheering him on before humping his leg like a nympho.

And that kiss had been something else entirely. She grinned as she stretched in her bed, kicking the covers off and lying there, spread-eagled in her Spongebob short set.

Yes, that kiss had made her forget any other man that had been in her life, it had reduced her hormones to their basic form and made her ovaries do little victory dances in her abdomen If she could, she would have crawled up his body like a pole dancer, but she had some self-restraint.

How she had managed to detangle herself from him and walk away she had no idea, but she deserved a medal. That would most definitely be the last time she took on one of Barbie's challenges. Although, Barbie had seemed very proud of her and how she pulled it off.

Her issue now was getting over that kiss. Yes, it was just a kiss, but somehow, deep inside, she felt it meant more, that somehow it was the start of something that would change her life completely. She still had that huge level of mistrust, thanks to Russell, but - and it was a huge but - Barbie had been right. She was lonely, and she really did want to get back on the horse, and if the mammoth of a man that kissed liked sin was game, then so was she.

Rolling out of bed, Andromeda went in search of coffee and her mobile phone, the first one to wake her up, the second one to check in with the world. Her business was her number one priority, not some guy with lips that could make her knees quake and her stomach roll.

A girl could daydream though, right?

Chapter Eight

Monica Bailey smiled at the lady in front of her as she slowly turned over the cards. Her client's face only showed awe and excitement; the idea of having your future read was becoming a craze. Not that she minded, the new influx of customers meant she had more money than before, but a lot of customers had no idea what they were getting themselves into. Most didn't believe in what she did and used it as a joke with their friends. Dealing with the energies of the cosmos was no laughing matter.

Turning over another card, Monica fought a wince as her client, Kimberley, screeched.

"Death! Oh, my god, I'm going to die, aren't I? Oh no!"

The urge to roll her eyes and smack Kimberley upside the head was strong, but Monica was stronger. Forcing the brightest smile she could, she reached over and took the young lady's hand.

"Shush, it's ok, you are not going to die." She waited for the girl to calm before she continued, "Your death is not revealed to me. I cannot say when or how, but as with all things in life, it ends."

"Really? But you pulled the death card, doesn't that mean death is going to happen?"

Monica shook her head. "No, dear, it doesn't always mean death, it can mean the end of a journey, change and rebirth."

Kimberley merely nodded, but she had started to smile again now that the prospect of imminent death had been avoided. Monica continued to explain the meaning of the cards to her, keeping as close to her question as possible. Never in her years of reading had Monica had a day like this one. Finishing the reading and bidding Kimberley goodbye, she finally closed the door on her small caravan. It was miles apart from opulence of her house back when she was with her husband, but she loved how cosy it was even if she invited strangers in every day.

Today's energies felt off, like they were on a tilt. Every single reading she had done today had dealt the same set of cards. Six out of every set were exactly the same. That never happened. Every reading was usually as unique as the client having it. Today they almost screamed to be heard.

Moving back to her table, Monica gently put the tarot cards away, wrapping them in silk and placing them in a small wooden box. She wouldn't use her everyday cards now, she would use her own personal ones, ones that had aided her with every step of her life. These had helped her deal and find a direction when she had been left a single mum, completely heartbroken from the death of the love of her life. They had given her the courage to live her life to the fullest. Most would scoff at the fact some small cards had done all this, but unless they were in her shoes they would never understand.

Lifting a hand, she reached into the shelf that was above her table and pulled out the small bag that was hidden in the dark corner. The velvet rubbed against her skin and caused goose bumps to erupt. Tingles vibrated over her fingers as she opened the bag and pulled the small worn deck from its hiding place. The edges were dog-eared, the colour darkened with age, but they were loved and the energies, to her, always felt right. Monica seated herself and closed her eyes as her hands slowly shuffled the cards. She centred herself, emptying her mind,s letting the energies and the will of the cards tell her their story.

Her fingertips rubbed against the worn cards as she slowly pulled six from the stack and placed them in the common star spread. This only required six cards in total, so if the same came up again, she would know her gut-feeling was right.

One card after another revealed themselves.

Death

The Devil

Three of Swords

Five of Wands

Two of Cups

Five of cups.

Exactly that same cards that had been making an appearance all day. Their meaning to Monica was crystal clear. Change was coming, that was certain, but she somehow knew it wouldn't be her that was on the receiving end of those changes. Standing again, Monica pulled a small amethyst pendant from her pocket, attached to it was a long silver chain. This had been her first and only scrying crystal and had never failed her. The only reason she was doing this now was to confirm if the cards were speaking about her or about someone else. To be honest, it would be easier to deal with if they were warning her about her own future, but knowing fate, it wouldn't be so easy or simple.

Monica didn't waste any time in pulling out a large rolled-up map that was under the sofa of her van and spread it out over the dining table. She had multiple maps for when people asked her to search for a lost relative, or even a dog, but this one showed the city of Manchester. Every town that made up the city was shown, along with the streets. Once again, she closed her eyes and centred herself, letting her gift come forward. Holding out the crystal, she hung it over the map.

Within seconds the crystal started to circle, the arch growing bigger and bigger as the energies flowed through it, before they started to reduce in size. Monica felt the pull on her hand, guiding her to its chosen location, and went with it, keeping her eyes closed until she felt the crystal-point hit the map.

Deep down inside, Monica knew where it would be, but still, her heart dropped as she found the crystal-point on the exact location of her daughter's new shop.

The hairs on her arms raised and she felt a cool breeze at her neck. It had only been days – or was it weeks – ago that she had dealt cards of a similar nature, but she had ignored them after Andromeda had told her all was well. Clearly a mistake on her part.

The fates had plans for her Andromeda, plans Monica dreaded. Silently, she prayed to whatever gods were listening that her daughter would be watched over and safe. She had to believe in fate and the strength of heart and soul. Because when the fates got involved, there was little else to do but ride it out until the end.

Hades sat at the dining table in Arianna and Arcaeus's home and watched as the girls practically squealed in delight and the males just smirked after he had told them about the kiss. They had ignored the fact that it had been a game for his soulmate and she hadn't wanted to kiss him but had been dared to kiss the next person to walk through the door. His gut tightened at the thought of her kissing anyone else but him.

"So, is she pretty, is she what you expected?" Sonia the red-head asked. She, out of the two, was always the more direct with her questions.

"Indeed she is, she is better than my imagination," he stated simply, gaining a strange look from both the males. If he didn't know them any better, he would say they were making fun of him, but he had seen how they looked at their own soulmates. As much as they wanted to be all manly and tough, they would do anything for the girls in front of him. Both had already given the ultimate sacrifice of their lives, and would no doubt do so again.

That was how he felt about his soulmate, he always had, ever since that first day of seeing her in Elyssia. His heart and soul had decided for him, ignoring the warning in his head that it would only end in pain. The pain part had been true; there were only so many years a man could watch his love enter the fields and not know him. But that had been his fault, he had never left the underworld to find her. Maybe if he had, she would have known him, and maybe, just maybe, would have stayed in the underworld with him. But what kind of life would that have been? As much as having her by his side would have been a dream come true, they would still be missing that one aspect that, in all honesty, Hades craved.

Touch.

He wanted to hold his mate in his arms, kiss her sweet lips, stroke her skin, lose himself in her depths.

Maybe this would be his chance.

"So, stop daydreaming and tell us more about her," Arianna enthused. Both girls looked eager to know any and all information he had, but he felt a reluctance to share.

"She is beautiful, with hair the colour of the light that shines from the stars in Elyssia, so white it's almost silver, with a slight hint of gold. Eyes so pale they rival the most perfect aquamarine gemstone ever found." He could go on and on about her perfection, but he wouldn't, he would keep the rest locked away in his mind like a treasured memory until he was able to create more with her.

His heart swelled at the prospect of learning more about his Andromeda. Her name fit her beauty. She was his siren, his curse… His.

And he would move both worlds to have her by his side. But it was all well and good saying it, the hard part was making it a reality.

"So, what's the plan, then?" Arcaeus called out from the kitchen, his dark eyes almost reading Hades' mind.

"Well," Hades started, but his voice was soon drowned out by the girls as they came up with idea after idea of getting Andromeda to meet him.

"Andromeda Bailey," Cosmos added, "Is that her name?"

Hades looked blank. Shit, that was a great start, wasn't it? All they knew was her first name.

"That is correct, Cosmos," a new voice chimed in.

Aphrodite walked into the room and was engulfed by the hugs of both Arianna and Sonia.

Cosmos nodded and went back to looking at his phone. Hades would have to purchase one of those. That would be something he would discuss with the goddess later on.

"Ok," Cosmos started, and everyone fell silent. "Andromeda Bailey is the owner of the new jewellery shop about ten minutes' walk away. She only does commissions as she handmakes everything herself. Maybe you could go commission something?"

"Excellent plan, Cosmos," Aphrodite responded. "What do you think, Hades? Are you game?"

Hades just smiled and nodded. His mate had a gift. She always had in her previous lives yet this one - where she was able to craft pieces of beauty and passion - suited her better than all others, and suited the lives they would have in the underworld together. There she would have access to stones of the rarest purity, and he would give her them all.

"Yes, I am game, as you say."

"Excellent," Aphrodite exclaimed, and clapped her hands before turning to Arianna. "So, my priestess, when is the baby due?"

Her question was met with silence from all except Arcaeus, who, in true male fashion, dropped the cup he was carrying and stood, mouth wide open, staring at Arianna.

"You're pregnant?" he asked quietly. Arianna nodded and looked almost frightened at him finding out.

"When? How?"

Cosmos snorted and moved so he could hold his own mate in his arms. "I think we all know how, Arcaeus, my friend."

"I wanted to tell you, but you made it clear you were happy how we are." Arianna lowered her eyes and even Hades could see the tears fall.

"Have I been that much of an arse?"

"Obviously" Sonia answered, and Hades looked at Aphrodite, who just shrugged. This was another mortal affair Hades had no idea how to deal with.

"I'm sorry." Arcaeus moved to stand in front of Arianna. Taking her hands in his, he slowly dropped to his knees, his eyes in line with her stomach. "How far along?" he asked.

"Ten weeks," she answered, but didn't elaborate.

"We're going to have a baby…" He then grinned up at Arianna, pulling her against him so he could kiss her tummy. "You are going to be a spoilt little bean, and I can't wait to meet you."

Hades felt uncomfortable. He felt he was

intruding on a special event that he hadn't been invited to. Knowing he wouldn't be missed for the time being, he vanished quietly, getting ready to make plans for his meeting with his own mate. Yet that feeling of wanting what the mortals had wouldn't leave him. Even the baby part. Would that be possible? He hoped so. There would be only one way to find out.

Chapter Nine

Persephone, goddess of the… Wait, what was she goddess of again? Other than being a simply amazing creature. Her mother was goddess of the harvest, so she was supposed to do something that tied in with that, but it had been centuries since she had got involved. That may have been why her mother was again pushing for her to align herself with one of the gods, an elder god, to be exact.

She didn't have the time nor the patience to deal with pushy mothers and broody gods. Apollo had been perfect for her, but she had grown tired of his obsession to seek revenge on the mortals when there were much more enjoyable things to do. Like take over Olympus and become the queen she deserved to be, with mortals, as well as the other gods, bowing at her perfectly manicured feet.

So, she had left Apollo in his purgatory like he deserved. She would free him when she was queen, but for now, she would keep an eye on him there. The next step was to seduce an elder god, and that was the hardest part. Zeus had been MIA ever since the silly trout, Aphrodite, had got herself all tied up with the energies, and he had spent more and more time away with the elder Oracle. The only thing that managed to do was annoy Hera, who, once again, thought he was off seducing maidens. But then again, Hera was gullible, she always had been. It hadn't taken much to make her think he had cheated on her. Thanks to Persephone, there was no heir to the throne of Olympus, and there wouldn't be in the future as Hera had banned Zeus from her bed. But alas, Persephone had been unable to seduce him. Turns out that the elder god, although banished from his wife's bed, had remained true. Those idiots actually loved each other but were so blind they believed everyone else instead of their own hearts. It really was laughable.

Then came her attempt on Poseidon. Anyone would think that god would be foaming at the bit for some female company after holing himself under the sea for so long. Nope, that miserable git hadn't even let her in his domain. That left Hades, the one god she had rejected all those years ago in her shallow youth. He had no trust for her, and she didn't blame him. She just had to work harder to bring him around and make him see that she was the perfect option for him.

So, here she was, deep in the depths of the earth, making a house call to the creatures that Hades had banished when the gods had become gods.

Three sisters, so ugly that Persephone felt bile rise in her throat. The fates, keepers of the gates to the cosmos and dealers in death.

Why was Persephone here? Well, she wanted a heads-up on how to tie Hades to her, but ultimately, how to remove the competition and rule Olympus herself.

She would bring back the old days where mortals cowered and served the gods. Where they ruled all and were worshipped.

"Persephone, why come to the gates of creation?"

"I seek knowledge, dear sisters," she answered, and kneeled, although she cringed as her knees touched the filth on the floor. Things moved in the shadows that made her skin crawl with revulsion.

"What knowledge do you seek?" one sister asked, her head tilting. The hole where her eyes should be were gaping and oozing, and her skin was pocketed, some parts decaying away. They were neither alive nor dead. They had been beautiful once, all three desired by any man that would look at them, even the gods had been tempted. But every time they used their powers, that beauty ebbed away. The price for being the keepers of fate was high, yet they embraced it. With one eye between the three, they knew all, saw all. They didn't care that over the millennia they slowly faded into creatures unrecognisable as women. Frail to behold, greying, rotting, brittle skin. Hideous yet powerful.

"I want to be queen, queen of Olympus."

"Ahh, goddess, you ask much, the price for this is high." The second sister cackled, "Are you prepared?"

"I am, tell me what I need to do." Excitement thrummed through Persephone, soon her dreams would come true.

"Sacrifice," the third sister called out. "The sacrifice of a pure heart."

"Ha! Easy, that will be done."

"You will also need to gain the powers of an elder god," the sisters chimed in as one. "But tread carefully, Persephone, the god you chose is on a different path. He seeks his heart. Know that only death will come if you battle him outright."

"How do you know which god I was aiming for?" Persephone asked, and as soon as it left her mouth, she felt stupid. The fates knew everything.

"We know," they answered. "Just as we know the

path you have chosen sits on a narrow ledge of success. One small step either side and you will fail."

Persephone stood and brushed her dress down before she thrust her shoulders back, confidence filling her. "I will be the victor. His death and the death of those he loves will bring what I am owed. I will not lose."

She would do whatever it took to get her way, even if it meant murder. She grinned, Apollo had taught her well, and she was looking forward to testing her new skills.

She would take everything from Hades, all she had to find out was what he loved the most.

Chapter Ten

The soft strains of *A Midsummer Night's Dream* flowed through Andromeda's work room. The sounds of violins helped with her mood as she kept her head down and worked on her most recent commission. Her issue was - and it had been since Saturday - the kiss.

It was a kiss filled with so much promise that she hadn't been able to stop thinking about it, or about the owner of the lips that had caressed hers so exquisitely, since. Surely a man that skilled should be illegal or have a warning on him to let women like herself know that addiction was certain. She hadn't slept well either, her dreams had instead been filled with erotic images of things that usually came after a kiss like the one she had been a part of.

Barbie had enjoyed the aftermath as well. Knowing it had affected Andromeda, she had continuously brought it up. Andromeda shook her head but smiled at the memory of Barbie's inquisition on the evening of that mind-blowing kiss. If anything, Barbie had that unique ability to put even the most anxious and stressed person at ease.

"You liked it, didn't you?"

"Of course I liked it, Barbie, the guy could kiss, and he was hot as hell. Who wouldn't like it?" Andromeda smirked and knocked back her bottle of beer. It was either that or go back to the pub and jump on the helpless male she had already attacked once.

Barbie leaned in, her voice low as if parting a secret, "Did it make you wetter than an otter's pocket, Rommie?"

Andromeda just stared at her best friend. "What?"

"Was your lagoon dripping in anticipation?"

"Barbie! What the fuck?" Andromeda shook her head, ignoring the look of pure innocence from her friend. "You, my warped friend, have been reading far too many porn stories."

"You can never read enough porn, Rommie, and stop changing the subject. Did you want to dance the fandango with him?"

"Yes."

"Ha! I win."

"Fuck off."

"Ow, dammit!" Andromeda shouted as her lapse in concentration ended up with her slicing the thumb of her left hand open. The file she had been expertly using to shape and smooth a setting was now coated with blood. She moved away from her work station, careful to stop any blood falling on her project. Blood was one of the hardest things to remove from jewellery, especially intricate pieces that held stunning stones. It would get into the smallest of areas, leaching into gaps that she wouldn't be able to get to. Yes, there was the option of cleaning with an ultrasonic bath, but that took time away from finishing the piece, time she didn't necessarily have. At the moment, time was money, and she needed every single second.

Andromeda moved over to the sink and placed her thumb under the tap, cleaning the wound to see how bad it actually was. Bisecting her left thumb was an inch-long laceration. Andromeda winced as she squeezed her thumb, creating a fresh delivery of blood. Once she was sure there were no pieces of silver inside, she wrapped it tightly with a small hand towel. She hoped she could stop the bleeding and it would only require a plaster. Again, time at the hospital for a small cut would take time away from her shop, and she couldn't afford that.

"Hello," a voice called, a voice Andromeda had hoped she would never hear again.

Walking back out to the shop front and to her work station, Andromeda glared. "Russell, what the fuck are you doing here?"

Andromeda was not a violent person; she was more of a runaway kinda girl. But seeing the man that had caused her not only heartbreak but nearly destroyed her career, had her thinking of places that would be ideal for hiding a body. She already knew that Barbie would help.

"Now, now, angel, no need to be like that. I've just come to see how you are."

"I'm just peachy, now leave," she answered simply. She wanted to shout and scream, but she would be the better person and attempt to not have a mild tantrum.

She folded her arms across her chest and watched as her slime ball ex moved forward. She could tell he was looking for her designs. Back when they had been a couple, she had a habit of leaving them lying around, but she had learned her lesson. Now they were kept upstairs, out of the way of prying eyes. To be frank, she had expected him to come nosing a lot sooner. She was, after all, the gifted one in the relationship. It had been her work that had got the attention, only he had sold it off as his own.

"I'm glad you're ok. Can we talk?" he asked sweetly.

"No."

"Oh, come on, angel, for old times' sake."

"No," was her answer, when all she wanted to say was, *What happened to the blonde?* Instead, she kept it cool. Barbie would be proud.

"Angel…"

"Please stop calling me that. I don't like it and I want you to leave." Andromeda could feel herself start to shake. She wanted him to go, needed him to get out of her life.

"You used to like it." He smirked and moved to walk around the counter. Andromeda shook her head. She knew what he was trying to do, but her mind had gone blank with how to deal with him.

"I believe the lady asked you more than once to leave."

The deep voice that came from her doorway was a shock to her system, and she almost cried with relief. There, looking hotter than she remembered, was the guy she had kissed in the pub. He filled the doorway, dressed in jeans and a blue t-shirt, and stared coldly at Russell.

Andromeda looked at Russell, who had stopped his path around her work desk. Instead, he had his hands placed in his pockets, smiling at her and then at her visitor.

"This your new boyfriend, Rommie? Didn't take you long, did it?"

Andromeda was close to seeing red. Her heart thumped hard against her chest until she could hear it vibrate in her ears. Yet, she didn't deny who the guy was. Let Russell think what he liked.

"As opposed to you banging anything in a skirt while we were still together, Russell?" She sneered his name. "We both know you didn't give a shit, so do me a favour and leave."

Andromeda hadn't heard the guy move, but suddenly he was stood beside Russell. She would have laughed if she wasn't so angry. The size difference between the two was comical. Russell, with his pressed suits and dress shoes, who never worked out and was about as strong as Kermit the frog, next to a guy that looked like he could chest press a small car, and who filled his clothing like they had been painted on. It made her wonder what she had actually seen in her ex.

"Are you going to do what the lady asked or do I have to make you?" The guy's deep voice caused butterflies to erupt in her stomach. She had never been the damsel in distress kind of girl, but she was open to all options now, seeing as he was escorting her ex from her shop.

"I will see you again, Andromeda," Russell called out as he moved through the door, followed by a yelp. She grinned at the thought of Russell getting a good thumping, but then a part of her didn't want her saviour to get in trouble. Thoughts, though, became almost impossible as her knight in jeans and cotton walked back in. The impulse to do what she had been thinking of Saturday night came back full force.

Just the sight of his tall, muscled body had her wanting to climb him like a… What had she thought? Oh right, she had wanted to use him as a pole for her dancing. Had? Hell, she still did. Who wouldn't?

"Are you ok?" he asked, and her body reacted like he had touched her. A shiver travelled up her spine and caused the hair on the back of her neck to stand.

Andromeda nodded, her voice not quite ready to function yet. She watched as he walked closer, moving around her work bench until he stood right in front of her.

"Let me see," he said quietly, and it took longer than it should for her to realise he was talking about her hand. Not a word left her mouth as he reached down and picked up her left hand. He gently pulled the towel away from where it was wrapped around her thumb. The bleeding had stopped, but she had to hold in a yelp of pain as his large hand investigated the wound.

"This is deep," he said, and his eyes met her own. Again, all she could do was nod in response.

"Should you not seek a healer?" he asked, and Andromeda's mind finally caught up.

"A healer? You mean a doctor?" she asked weakly.

"Yes."

"It will be fine. I can't leave the shop just to sit in A&E for the whole day, and they would probably send me home with just a plaster on it anyway." She looked up into his deep, dark eyes, and that strange sense of déjà vu hit her again. She had only met him once before today yet she felt she had known him longer.

He nodded and released her hand. "Let me help you, then?"

"Ok," she breathed out, and moved past him so she could go back to the sink. With her free hand, she pulled the first aid kit from the shelf above. Holding the green box out, she waited for him to take it from her. She didn't miss the flash of confusion as it flickered across his face.

"If you could take out the sterile wipes and the steri strips for me…"

Hades looked at the contents of the box and then back up to Andromeda, this was not what he had been expecting to do when he'd finally got away from the mortal's home and made his way here. But she needed his help, so he would try and figure out what she wanted and attempt to not make himself look a total fool.

He could, in fact, heal her straight away, but that would raise questions that he wasn't ready to answer. So, Hades bent his head and looked into the box, reading the labels carefully, hoping they would identify what she had asked for. Pulling out a small packet, he held it out and at the same time held his breath. When she took it and smiled, he released it, thankful he had been lucky and given her the right item. Then he looked through the box for an item she called steri strips. He had absolutely no clue what they were or what they looked like. The last time he had been in the mortal realm for longer than a night, the idea of something small patching up a wound was unheard of. The battles that had raged ended up with more than a laceration, more along the lines of missing limbs or disembowelment.

"The blue packet," Hades heard her say, and immediately grabbed it and handed it over. He then placed the box on the worktop next to the sink and watched as she quickly cleaned then placed the strips over the wound to close the gap.

"Thank you," she stated while she cleaned up the sink and threw what she hadn't used into the bin. "Thank you for getting rid of Russell."

"He was bothering you and he wouldn't leave when you had asked him to. That was not honourable," Hades said. This Russell had been lucky to only get thrown out onto the street. Ideally, Hades would have liked to inflict a little more damage, especially after hearing the way he spoke to Andromeda and what he had said. This male had hurt her, there would be no way Hades would allow that ever again.

"He's an arsehole," she stated before she turned and leaned back against the sink, her arms folded once again across her chest and her hair that was braided like he remembered hung over her shoulder. What he wouldn't give to be able to slowly unravel the braid, taking his time to run his fingers through the soft locks before he pulled her against him and…

"So, what can I help you with?" Her voice broke through his thoughts.

"What?"

"Was there a reason you came to my shop?" she asked, and Hades remembered the plan the mortals had helped him with.

"Yes, my apologies. My name is Hades…" Hades coughed and remembered the other name he was supposed to use. "My name is Haden, and I have heard excellent reviews about your work and would like to commission a piece."

Hades watched as, at first, Andromeda frowned, then moved from her place by the sink. She slowly walked past him and Hades felt like she was annoyed with him. He didn't have a clue why she would be, he had just helped rid her of an annoyance. Following her into the shop, he paused and then sat in the chair that she stood pointing at.

"Ok, what would you like, a ring, necklace, bracelet?"

What did he want? Hell, this part he had totally forgotten about, he had been more focused on getting into the shop and speaking to her.

"I would like a torque making, one set with fire

opals and black onyx." Hades smirked, he would bet Cerberus's heads that she hadn't expected that.

"A torque? As in a Viking style choker?"

Hades nodded.

"With fire opals and black onyx?"

"Yes, can you do this?"

"In silver, gold, or platinum?"

"Silver would be perfect, and please don't copy anything Viking, I would prefer something with a Greek twist."

"It may take me a while to source the stones."

Hades stood and reached into his back pocket. Pulling out a small velvet pouch, he handed it over and smiled. "No need, there should be enough stones for the piece in there, and whatever you don't use you may keep."

He watched as Andromeda opened the pouch and emptied it onto a velvet pad on her desk. The oranges, reds, and golds of the opals fired under the shop lights and the black onyx drew in the warmth. A perfect contrast.

"Oh, wow," she breathed. "These are stunning."

"Yes," Hades uttered. "I couldn't agree more." But he wasn't speaking about the stones. His eyes had never left Andromeda's face. He couldn't wait to see her wearing the stones.

"Ok, I will start with a design. Would you like to come back, say, in a week, to discuss it?"

A week. Hades frowned, that would not do at all. He was an impatient god and wanted her to start straight away. He didn't want to wait a week to see her again.

"Can you not start straight away? I will compensate you accordingly," he asked, trying to keep the impatience he felt from his voice.

He scanned Andromeda's face as she sat back in her chair, her eyes fixed on the stones. He hoped that she felt the pull to him just the same as he felt it to her.

Finally, after what felt like hours, she returned her gaze to his own and nodded. "Yes, I will start right away." She blushed bright red but continued "Would you be able to meet me later on to discuss the design?"

Hades grinned. That was something he had wanted to suggest but had been afraid of pushing her too fast.

"Yes, perfect," he answered, this time not hiding the excitement he felt. "How about we go somewhere for food as well?"

Andromeda bit her lip, looking uncertain. Hades felt blessed, once again, that his mate was such a stunning, expressive creature, but watching her bite her lip was doing things to his libido that would most definitely scare her off so soon in the courting.

"Ok, where do you want to go?" she asked shyly.

Now this was something he had neglected to ask the mortals. "You choose. I do not know the tavernas that well around here."

"Tavernas? You mean restaurants," she corrected, and stood. She collected the stones and gently placed them back into the velvet pouch.

"Ahh yes, restaurants." Hades smiled. "Shall we say around seven tonight?"

"Ok," Andromeda agreed. "I will see you then."

Hades bowed low, crossing his right arm across his chest.

"Until tonight." His voice had deepened, but he didn't care. With one final look, he turned and left the shop, more hopeful than he ever had been.

Chapter Eleven

"So, you have a date?" Barbie's voice sing-songed over the phone. Andromeda had left it on speaker as she perched on the lid of the toilet, attempting to shave her legs.

"It's not a date, woman. How many times do I have to say that? We are meeting to discuss a custom design he has asked me to do."

"Yeah alright, and I'm the sugar plum fairy. Rommie, this is the same dude you snogged in the pub, that can't be a coincidence, not in Manchester where hot men are rarer than a man with a full set of nashers."

"I think you're letting your poor choice of date cloud the issue, Barbie. There are quite a few hot men here."

"Most are gay, bloody lucky bastards, if you ask me," Barbie grumbled. "They could at least save some for us. I've said as much to Henry."

"And what did your gay best friend have to say to that?" she asked, although Andromeda knew what was coming.

"Apparently, according to Mr perfect, I don't deserve them." She huffed, her sigh loud, making Andromeda smile. Whilst Barbie was a bit of a tart, she was lovable, and had been shit on more than a few times in the past. Most men couldn't handle her personality or would try to boss her around. One day, Andromeda hoped, both of them would finally meet someone that would be perfect for them.

"Stop trying to change the subject, Rommie, tonight is a date, just admit it."

"No, I won't, because if I did, now would be the time to start panicking."

"You're shaving your legs, aren't you?"

"Yes, but what's that got to do with anything?"

"You only shave them if you think you've got a chance, and you like the guy, Rommie. You forget, we are buds, I know you."

"Shut up," Andromeda answered with no heat in her voice. Barbie was right, she was hopeful, and the shaving of the legs was her tell sign that the meeting would turn into a date. At that thought, her phone vibrated as a text came through.

"What was that?" Barbie called out on the speaker.

"A text," Andromeda answered. Without ending the call, she checked her messages.

Andromeda,

I won't be able to make tonight at 7pm as something has come up unexpectedly. I apologise profusely. I was looking forward to spending more time with you and to discuss the torque.

Are you available tomorrow? Please say yes.

If you prefer, please bring a friend so you feel more comfortable. I will bring one also.

Haden x

"So, who was it?" Barbie asked. "Talk to me, I hate it when you go quiet."

"It was him, Haden. He can't do tonight."

"Oh, honey, I'm sorry. Shaving for nothing."

"But he wants to meet me tomorrow and says I can bring a friend and he will also. Strange, why didn't he just say double date?" Andromeda was confused by the message, it didn't sound like just a business meeting, it sounded along the lines of a date. She had mixed emotions. On the one hand, she was sort of relieved, she could relax a bit now and not rush to get ready. As much as she openly denied it, she did want to make an impression on Haden. On the other hand, she was gutted, she had already played the whole meeting out in her head, and it had ended with a kiss, just like the one in the bar, only this one was more passionate.

"Yes, I will be your wing woman," Barbie screeched through the phone, and Andromeda laughed.

"Of course you will. So, tomorrow night, get here and we can get ready together."

"Ahhhhh, a double date. It's been a while. Now piss off, I have some serious grooming to do. You know, legs, armpits, moustache… Oh, and not forgetting my area of outstanding natural beauty."

"Ugh. Bye, Barbie, have fun."

"Laters."

Andromeda shook her head as the phone went dead. Picking it up, Andromeda responded to the message, trying to play it cool.

Haden,

I hope everything is ok, thanks for letting me know. Tomorrow is fine with me, and I will bring a friend. I look forward to seeing you.

Andromeda

She kept it simple, not wanting to sound desperate, needy, or just strange. Putting her phone back onto the shelf, she carried on with the grooming. She would finish up and then go back to her design board. She wanted to tweak the design for the torque and make it perfect.

Hades couldn't help himself from constantly checking his new phone. The shiny object in his hands would take some getting used to, but he would adapt and conquer, as he always did. Although it had taken him four - or was it five? - attempts to type out the message to Andromeda. In the end, he had gotten Hermes to do it. Much to his distaste.

Hermes would no doubt use this to try to piss him off. With Zeus still AWOL, it was left to him to be Hermes' sole purpose of annoyance.

"Haven't you got some mortal to annoy?" he snapped. Hermes had spent the last ten minutes sat in a chair, grinning at him. He said nothing, just grinned, and for some unknown reason, that had started to annoy the ever-living shit out of him.

Instead of answering, Hermes just grinned even more.

"Arsehole," Hades muttered, and stood from his chair. They were currently in the outer chamber of Aphrodite's temple. Hermes had done his job and summoned Hades, which messed with his plans as he had a 'date' and now he had had to use that stupid device to postpone the meeting with his mate. That annoyed him more than anything. They didn't have time to waste sitting in a temple.

"Where is she?" he growled, and watched as a nymph bolted for the exit.

"Grumpy bastard, aren't we?"

"Fuck off."

"What's made you all sour, you not getting anywhere with your mate?"

"I suggest you shut up, Hermes."

"Or what?"

Before he could answer with a nice description of what he would do to the lesser god, Aphrodite made her entrance.

"Or I will do something you both will regret." Her voice carried around the whole temple, but it wasn't its usual melodic sound. Instead, it sounded strained.

"What's happened?" Hades asked.

"I will tell you all, and it shouldn't take long to rectify, and then we can get you sorted for your double date," she answered, and smiled.

"Hermes has agreed to go with you," she continued, but frowned when Hades shook his head.

"No, not happening. I am not going anywhere with him."

Hermes now stood, his own features not happy. "And why the fuck not?"

"Because you are a twat and I don't want you anywhere near my mate."

"Then who will accompany you, Hades. You can't take Cosmos or Arcaeus."

Aphrodite paced before she moved to the alcove where her companion, Meton, perched, preening his feathers.

"Meton can," Hades called.

"What? How will that work when he is an eagle, Hades."

Hades smirked. "I can explain later, once we have returned. Are you going to tell me where we are going and why?"

Aphrodite nodded. "Your charge has found a way to access the mortal realm and he's after the Essence." She kept it brief before she turned and headed for the exit.

Hades' mind whirred like a cog in an engine.

"Essence… As in Cupid?"

All Aphrodite did was nod before she left the room, and all Hades could do was follow.

Chapter Twelve

Andromeda lay in a field of brightly coloured flowers. Overhead, the blue sky was clear but for a few scattered clouds, wisps that moved quickly with the light breeze. The sun's ray warmed her skin and she couldn't help but close her eyes and stretch. Her arms above her head, she basked in the sun's attention.

Her dress, one made of the finest silk, clung to her skin as it heated and became damp. Tendrils of her hair that had escaped its confines stuck to her cheeks, refusing to move.

She felt at ease and at peace. All was right in her world, all was perfect.

Until a dark cloud passed ahead, blocking out the sun and its warmth. Andromeda opened her eyes to see it wasn't a cloud but another person. A handsome man stood before her; blonde hair, blue eyes, yet his smile was cold and unfeeling.

A sense of warning made Andromeda move. She sat

up only to find the man upon her in an instant, pushing her back down. His smile was gone and replaced by a sneer, his eyes blazing with fury and greed.

"You have fobbed me off one to many times, Eliza. No more."

"Get off me, Alexis." Andromeda found her mouth moving, but she had no control over what came out.

"No, you are mine and I will take what I am owed."

"Over my dead body," she spat out, and at the same time her hand whipped up, slapping the man – Alexis - across the face. For a moment, it was as if time had stopped. His face showed only shock that she had indeed raised a hand to him, but fear of what he would do next made her move. Sliding her feet from under him, she turned, ready to bolt back to the safety of her home which lay just over the brow of the hill, only his hand wrapped around her ankle, stopping her movement.

"You will pay for that," he spat into her ear, and he pressed her against the floor, his own body preventing any movement. She squirmed in an attempt to move, even when she felt his hand slide up her calf and under her dress.

Her heart stopped and then raced, she would fight this fate until her dying breath. No man would take her innocence until she was ready to give it. She tilted her head forward and then thrust it back with as much force as she could muster. A sense of triumph, although short-lived, raced through her when she heard bone crunching and his yell of pain. Digging her fingers into the grass, she pulled herself from under his body once again. Freedom was within grasp, and then she would tell all whom she knew exactly what Alexis O'Connor was, and it wasn't a man of honour.

A shout and then numbness - or was it shock - flowed through Andromeda's body. Her limbs no longer responded. A dull ached started in her skull but then blossomed into blinding pain that took away her breath and the ability to talk.

"You will never run from me, if I cannot have you as mine then no one else will." His cruel laugh cut through, straight to Andromeda's heart. He was killing her. It didn't surprise her; he was that type. She had heard the rumours. She felt her body jerk as another blow to the head was delivered. Andromeda felt nothing. In a daze-like state, she watched him circle her, dropping the large rock he had used. His voice was more muffled now, and she was unable to make out words.

She was dying and she didn't mind. She would be free from animals like Alexis who thought a woman was nothing more than a possession that he could use as he liked. She was free from men like her father who assumed that because she was female, she knew nothing. She was free.

Andromeda closed her eyes and felt her body lift.

She was free, free to find the man with the royal blue eyes.

The man that greeted her every time she died.

"What the fuck?" Andromeda called out loud as she sat up in bed. Sweat covered her entire body, making her shorts and t-shirt stick to her like a second skin. Her hair that had managed to unravel itself from its braid now surrounded her like a curtain. Just like in the dream, the tendrils stuck to her face, refusing to move. Looking at her bedside clock, it read 3:20 a.m. She had been asleep only a few hours yet had once again managed to have another strange as hell dream. A dream that ended the same as all the others, with her dying. Only it wasn't her as such, her consciousness was her, but her body and looks were that of someone else.

She threw back the covers and got up. There was no getting back to sleep at this point, there never was. The only consolation to her dodgy sleeping pattern was that it seemed to be her most creative time. She had, in the past, come up with her best designs between the hours of three and six a.m.

Andromeda reached for her pencils and drew,

losing herself to her design. She let her imagination flow into her drawing, the silence only broken by the scratch of pencil on paper, until she found herself staring at a torque, one that even she had to admit looked far too complicated to create.

But that, in itself, was a challenge, and one she would rise to and dominate, as she always had.

The original design she had made to show Haden was nothing compared to this. Each piece of silver twisted together in an intricate pattern, making way for the gemstones that the vines cupped as if they were floating. This allowed light to filter in behind and would make the stones fire.

By the time it was finished, it was seven a.m. Andromeda would have to open her shop in another couple of hours. Placing her pencil back on the table, she stood and walked to her sofa. She would get another hour's sleep and then take on the day. Her mind seemed less troubled now she had the design finished and it didn't take long for sleep to claim her.

"So, explain again to me how my companion, who is an eagle, is going to accompany you on a double date," Aphrodite's voice called out to Hades as he stood looking out over Olympus.

Meton was curious about that as well, it had been a long time since he had been in the form of a human, and even then he had been only a child. What would having legs again be like?

"We change him of course. Seriously, goddess, I do wonder sometimes… Is your head full of glitter or is that just Cupid?" Hades always seemed quite grumpy to Meton, but now he understood why. The fact that the goddess had asked such a simple question actually surprised him, usually she was ahead of the game. His reference to Aphrodite's creation irked Meton a little, but then again, he would admit that deity was not a patch on his goddess, and he *was* a little bit on the crackers side.

"But…"

"But what, goddess? It's a simple plan and he won't be human forever, just long enough to help me in this human ritual, date… thing."

"I didn't know he could be human again," she said quietly. "I changed him when he was but a young boy and I thought the fact it had been centuries since he had been human would prevent it."

Hades shook his head and smiled. "No, not at all."

Meton just looked back and forth. Nice how he wasn't really being consulted on this, but he wouldn't be protesting. He wanted to be human again, even if only for a moment, so he could maybe, just maybe, hold her hand, stroke her cheek. It didn't take an Oracle to know that Meton had been in love with the goddess of love since she had rescued him. At first, it had been young infatuation and gratitude, but over the many, many years, it had grown. He would do anything for his goddess. She was so focused on saving everyone else's love lives she barely had a spare thought for her own. Not that she would want him. She saw him as a companion only, nothing more, nothing less.

"Meton, are you ready?" Hades called out.

On swift wings, Meton flew to the centre of the room and landed gently on the floor. "My lord." He bowed to Hades and then to his lady. "My goddess, I am ready to help in whatever way I can."

"Brilliant. Let us begin, we don't have long."

Meton didn't have time to wonder as his eagle body was encompassed in a blinding blue light. Heat travelled through his body, leaving pins and needles in its wake. Then pain, burning pain erupted through his limbs and head before darkness took over.

Aphrodite gripped her chair until her knuckles turned white. Meton's cries of pain had her wanting to be by his side, but she couldn't interfere with the energies. Had they even asked if he was ok with this or just presumed that he would be? That had been rude and disrespectful of her. He was her companion, but also her closest friend. He had been there for her when there had been no one else.

As the light pulsed then ebbed, Aphrodite's breath caught. On the floor of her temple was no longer the form of a great golden eagle but now a large, naked man. His head was covered with golden hair and his skin was lightly tanned.

Standing, she approached cautiously. "Meton," she called, and was stopped by Hades.

"Give him time to come around, it will take some getting used to."

She waited as Meton slowly stood, his height reaching six feet easily. With his back to her, she could see that, just like in all the ancient Greek statues, he was all defined muscle. She was in awe of what Hades had done, until Meton turned around.

Aphrodite's mouth went dry and she lost the ability to speak. Meton, her one true friend, was gorgeous. His eyes were golden, just like they had been in his eagle form, but his face was like it had been sculpted from her own dreams. High cheek bones, stubborn chin, and lips that caused her gaze to drift to them every second.

"My lady." He bowed in front of her and her eyes struggled to take everything in. He was naked and glorious from the top of his head all the way down to his feet. She tried to avoid looking at his cock, but she hadn't been able to stop herself. He was perfect there, too. So perfect she felt her body respond. It had been a long time since she had even contemplated taking a lover, and then Hades goes and does this. Trying to school her thoughts, Aphrodite nodded in return.

"Meton, you look different." Inside, she wanted to crawl into a hole. Of course he looked different, he had been a damn eagle and now he was a man. Instead of correcting herself, she smiled and waved a nymph forward to hand him a covering. Although she could have quite happily had him naked constantly.

"Meton, thank you for your help," Hades called out. "Come, now we must leave; we must get ready for this date."

In any other circumstance, Aphrodite would have giggled at Hades trying to understand why a date was important, but now all she could think about was the other woman getting to put her hands on Meton.

Aphrodite had never felt jealously before, and she was surprised by its power. But she had no claim to Meton, he was, after all, her companion and no doubt had zero feelings for her anyway.

With that, she moved further into her temple as the males left, yet she couldn't shake the hurt that she felt in her heart.

Chapter Thirteen

Cupid sat back on the wooden bench and stretched his arms out above his head. A light breeze whispered through his golden locks and caressed his tanned skin. Once again, the mischievous god was dressed in his favourite ensemble; simple grey joggers - that was it. His bare chest was on show for all to see, and many looked. Who wouldn't; he was utter perfection and he knew it.

Luckily, there were not many present to question why a man was sat on a bench watching the ducks half-dressed, or why he had a silly smile plastered across his face as he looked passed the duck pond and to a restaurant that sat on its banks.

"Cupid?" the lyrical voice of Psyche called out from behind, causing Cupid's shoulders to stiffen slightly.

"Shit. Busted," he whispered to himself. "Ok,

Pedro, we got this," he mumbled, and then plastered a smile on his face.

Getting busted by his wife once again was not how he had planned this day to go. Ideally, he had wanted to complete his little plan and get back to their apartment in London before she had even realised he was missing. He had wanted to slide stealthily back into bed and nuzzle Pedro against her. She loved it when he did that. So did Pedro. However, she had become more and more suspicious of him after the recent events which had once again backfired on his toned, pert arse. They had even ended up calling in Aphrodite and Hades to help.

Just what he needed, family intervention. If he wasn't involved, he would have loved to sit back and watch Olympus's own version of Jeremy Kyle, especially with Zeus and Hera always fighting. The ratings would skyrocket with those two and a lie detector test.

Besides, what had happened before wasn't all his fault, the rogue and general pain in Olympus's arse, Apollo, had become involved and made the whole situation a lot worse.

Psyche had not been happy with him at all, and since then, she had been a tad distant with him. That was when she wasn't stalking him, as she was now.

"Darling love bug, I've missed you," he called out, and held out his arms, expecting her to run into them and lay some sugar on him. He adored his wife, always had and always would. She was the carrot to his cake, the ice to his berg, and in turn, he was the sausage to her roll. He had issues he was perfectly aware of, but she accepted him fully. Him and Pedro.

"Don't, Cupid," she said sharply. She stood about three feet away from him, and she didn't look happy.

"What?" he asked innocently.

"You know what! You vanished again, without telling me where you were going. What are you doing here?"

"Nothing," he answered, only to be given what he called the death stare. If his wife had been a Sith lord, she wouldn't have needed the force to kill people, that look alone would have done it. Darth Vader had sweet fuck all on Psyche. He chuckled to himself at his apt use of modern trivia.

"Cupid."

"Fine." Cupid huffed, knowing there was little point in lying or not answering. "I wanted to see Hades on his date."

"Is that all?" She had folded her arms and, as usual, that pulled his attention straight to her perfect, perky, dusky nipple-topped breasts.

"Mmmmm," he groaned, eyes glued on the prize, all the while licking his lips.

"For fuck sake, Cupid, concentrate," she snapped, and moved her arms so her breasts weren't pushed up and waving for his attention.

"No," he pouted, and not just a little pout. Nope, his bottom lip was hanging out so far you could have played a tune on it. "That's not all." Folding his own arms, he looked down and mumbled to his only friend, "I swear, Pedro, she teases us on purpose. I can't help but look at them. They are so, so boobish."

"So?" she asked, her voice strained from trying to remain calm.

"So, I wanted to give him a helping hand," Cupid replied, and looked up at Psyche, pushing his bottom lip out even more, opening his eyes wide and fluttering the lashes a little.

"Don't look at me like that, Cupid," she sighed. "I don't know whether to belt you around the ears or cuddle the shit out of you for being so damn adorable," she blurted. "You know you are not allowed to interfere."

"I can't interfere in mortals' lives, snookum's," he replied. The pouting lip vanished, replaced now with a smug grin. "Nothing was said about interfering in the gods' lives." He grinned as he corrected her before he stood to his full height and walked over.

"Let me play, just this once, my love. Hades deserves some action, and oh how entertaining this will be." Giving her his full-watt, sexy smile, he waited until she nodded, her own lips tilted a little as amusement started to set in.

"Fine. Just be careful, Cupid."

"I always am," Cupid answered, and leaned in for a swift kiss.

"Now, watch your sexy husband work." Before Psyche could stop him, Cupid reached out. Placing both palms over her breasts, he squeezed one then the other, all the while making honking noises.

She would admit that her life with Cupid, if not a tad stressful, had never been boring, and never would be.

Chapter Fourteen

Hades couldn't stand still as both Meton and himself waited outside the restaurant that Andromeda had chosen for their 'date'. His feet paced the pavement as Meton sat on a bench. Aphrodite's companion had said little since his change from eagle to human, all seemed to do was grunt and smirk.

Just like he was doing now.

"Why don't you just come out with it, Meton, instead of sitting there with that annoying smirk on your face."

"What do you want me to say, my lord?" Meton replied calmly.

Hades growled at the other male as he stalked past him, this date stuff was making him nervous. Gone were the days where females just flocked to be near him. But if he thought about it, did he want Andromeda to be like them?

No, he didn't. He liked her spirit, loved her ability

to cut through bullshit and be straight instead of fawning over him like the women he had dealt with in the past.

He had seen but a glimpse of her strength as she had stood up to her previous lover, watched as she had fought back any fear and doubt and defeated the situation. She was a warrior, and that appealed to him also. Never mind the fact he thought her more beautiful than Aphrodite herself. She roused his desire like no other, and ignited every protective instinct he owned. After only one meeting, he craved her company, wanted to be in her presence. In any other situation, he would have thought himself under the influence of one of Cupid's love potions, but he had been well prepared for his feelings when he had known he would meet his mate in the flesh instead of in Elyssia.

"Have you nothing to say about this date? Do you know what to expect? What happens?" Hades rushed out as he walked past Meton again.

"My lord, I have spent the past few hundred years, if not more, as a bird. I have never been on a date and, if I am honest, I haven't even kissed a woman, in this lifetime or my last. So, no, I haven't a clue as to what will happen or what to say."

Hades looked down at his present companion and

felt a twinge of guilt for his behaviour. It had slipped his thoughts that Meton had indeed dealt with his own issues. No one on Olympus but Aphrodite herself knew of what had gone on before she had returned from one of her trips to the mortal world with an eagle in tow. But the sadness and regret in Meton's eyes spoke volumes. A part of Hades wanted to pry, was eager to know his secrets, but he refrained. If he had learned any lessons from the mortals it was that, in their indefinite age, the gods had become rude and conceited. Demanding things they had no right to demand.

That was their legacy, that was how the mortals remembered them. Hades would not live up to that reputation, so he left Meton to his thoughts, quickly realising the conversation had stalled.

Hades stopped his pacing to close his eyes and tilt his chin up to the setting sun. A lot had happened since he had made the final decision to pursue his mate instead of watching her enter Elyssia time and time again. He had not only met the one destined for him, he had become almost friends with the mortals, started to wear mortal clothing, enjoyed a Costa coffee - though why the mortals went crazy after it, he didn't know - and then today, he had been taught how to drive. That had been an exhilarating experience. When Arcaeus and Cosmos had grinned as they described the speeds possible, he had been very dubious. Now he couldn't wait to get into the metal machine again. Maybe Andromeda would enjoy it.

That thought made him smile, he would enjoy every moment discovering every single small detail about her. He would learn her dreams, her fears, and conquer them for her as a mate and protector should.

As much as the idea of a date made him slightly nauseous, if it meant he got to spend more time with her, then he would embrace it. He looked back at the serious-faced Meton, wishing he had her to himself tonight and not 'double-dating', as Arianna had called it.

The sound of one of those metal machines had him turning to find the source, and when the noise abruptly stopped, he watched as Andromeda opened her door and got out, the fading sun gilding her hair. The sight of her had his heart racing and goosebumps rising, like a wave, down his body.

This was the first step to getting his mate.

Andromeda's knee bounced as she sat in the car with Barbie. Haden had caused this, was the catalyst to her being so nervous she was close to vomiting up the tiny lunch she had eaten. Her hands shook, and she had chewed her lower lip until there was a clear indent.

"Woman, quit that. You're shaking like a shitting dog!"

"I know, but I can't help it, I'm so bloody nervous."

"No shit, Sherlock," Barbie fired back as she eased the car into a parking space behind the restaurant. "I dunno why," she added.

"You know why," Andromeda answered, and gestured to the large, sexy as sin male that paced outside of the front of the building.

"Well damn, you never said he was He-man in disguise. He's huge." Barbie leaned forward and tilted her head from side to side. Andromeda knew she was mentally undressing him.

"Quit it, will you. Anyway, you saw him in the pub," Andromeda snapped, feeling a touch of jealousy. She hadn't even had the date with the guy yet and already she was feeling possessive. She couldn't deny the appeal Haden had; stacked with muscle, dark, brooding eyes. He was a walking wet dream.

"I've been hanging around with you far too much," she said to Barbie, only to get a grunt in response. Her focus shifted – thankfully - from Haden to his friend, who although not as tall and well built, was also drop-dead gorgeous.

Barbie was staring. In fact, she was almost drooling.

"Barbie, you've gone quiet on me."

"Shush. I'm thinking."

"About what?"

"My future and the role that hunk of love over there is going to play in it - and how I get into his pants."

Barbie's eyes were now glued to Haden's friend, and even as they got out of the car, she kept them on him. This eased Andromeda's fears and nervousness a touch. Maybe Barbie would make a fool of herself and take all the attention. Although, as she looked over at her date, she knew she wanted his sole attention on herself. He had noticed their arrival and was stood waiting. Dressed in all black, he looked dangerous yet so sexy that he seemed well out of her league.

Before Andromeda had even closed her door, Barbie was already shaking her date's hand and fluttering her eyelashes. In any other circumstance she would entertained by her best friend's actions, but she was too busy trying to calm her heart, which was thumping hard against her chest as her eyes met those of Haden's.

Her world tilted on its axis. Images - much like her dreams - assaulted her, flicking through her brain like an old-fashioned slide show. His eyes pulled her in, trapped her in their intensity and took her breath away. No man had ever done this with only a look before, and her heart doubled its pace as she imagined what it would be like to be at his mercy. She had only to step forward, one small step for the chance to find out. All she needed was courage.

She put one foot in front of the other, her heel clicking on the stone, then another, each step bringing her closer until, finally, she was stood in front of him. Their eyes had never parted.

"Andromeda." His voice sounded deeper than she remembered, but as he spoke each syllable of her name, her body reacted like he had physically touched her. She breathed his own name, surprised when he heard her.

He reached for her hand and raised it to his lips. The simple romantic gesture sent the hairs on the back of her neck upright and goosebumps raced over her skin. His scent, a deep aroma, teased her senses and heightened her awareness of him. All others were forgotten, and as he led her into the restaurant, she almost wondered if she would make it through the entire date without making a complete fool of herself. A part of her wanted Barbie and her date to leave them alone, but then the other part - the complete pussy - was scared to be left alone with a man who had her nerves and knickers in a twist.

Knickers in a twist or not, Barbie made the decision for them both and seated herself and her gorgeous date a few tables away. From the way she was babbling and fluttering her eyelashes, Barbie was more interested in Mr. Blue Eyes than helping her best friend not make a fool of herself.

"Andromeda." The way he said her name shot tingles down her spine. He enunciated every syllable, making her feel like she had the most exotic name ever created instead of a cheap knock-off from a Syfy programme.

"Have you thought more about the design?" he asked, and it took a few moments for her to register that he wanted to talk work. Grateful was an understatement, and she jumped on the subject, laying out every single plan she had for the torque. The gems he had provided would stand out perfectly on a silver background. With the gemstones being so large, she would struggle to keep it looking delicate, but that was a challenge she relished.

"I'm sorry, I'm rambling," she apologised, and blushed before she took a sip of the wine in front of her, savouring the crisp flavour as it settled on her tongue before sliding down her throat.

"No, please don't apologise. I enjoy hearing about your work, and it is obvious you are passionate about it. I made the right choice in asking you to commission the piece for me. You are very talented."

Andromeda nodded, not trusting herself to answer the compliment. Like any woman, she enjoyed them when given in earnest.

"You are so very beautiful, Andromeda," he said quietly so only she could hear it. Andromeda looked up from her glass, and once again, time stopped as their eyes met. She could swear she knew his eyes from somewhere, they were too familiar for it to be a coincidence.

"You think I'm beautiful?" she asked. Her ex had never said as much, just informed her that if she let herself go, he wouldn't stick around.

She watched as Haden leaned forward, his elbows resting on the table top as he moved to take both her hands in his. They seemed so small in his, a pale comparison to his tanned ones.

"Yes," he breathed. "More beautiful than the goddess of love herself." His honest answer gave

Andromeda butterflies, as did his thumb caressing her hand, focusing on the calluses she had from spending her time working with her tools. Her ex had hated them, telling her they made her hands manly, yet here was another man, caressing them.

A small cough had them separating and giving Andromeda the chance to breathe. Her smile died on her lips as she looked up into the face of yet another gorgeous male, one wearing a pair of joggers and a white apron that did nothing to hide his bare chest.

"Complimentary garlic bread for the romantic couple."

Andromeda's eyes snapped to her date as she heard a strange growing sound. Surely that wasn't him, was it?

"Eat, please eat. It was made just for you," the waiter encouraged. Andromeda obliged, smiling as she picked up a piece.

"Wait…" Haden called, but it was too late as she took the piece and bit into it.

After she had swallowed, she spoke. "Thank you, that was very kind."

"My pleasure," he answered, before locking eyes with Haden. "Have fun now."

"Everything ok?" she asked Haden as she wiped her lips on her napkin, only to crave more of the garlic bread provided. "Oh wow, this stuff is good. You need to try it."

With no more thought, Andromeda dived into the garlic bread like she would die without trying another piece.

Chapter Fifteen

Hades' knuckles cracked as he clenched his fists and watched Cupid bounce away. He had been unable to stop Andromeda from eating Cupid's little treat, and now he would be left dealing with the aftermath. He watched as his mate devoured the entire garlic bread almost like she had never eaten before. In no time at all, the garlic bread had vanished and his mate now sat with a dazed expression on her face. Hades knew what Cupid had done and, in a way, he was grateful. He may actually see Andromeda with her walls down. But he had wanted to court her properly and not be dealing with someone high on one of Cupid's love spells.

He watched as she lounged back in her seat, the smile on her face slow and erotic, causing his stomach to flip. Damn bloody Cupid, he wanted her to look at him like that without the need of a spell.

Only when a dainty, bare foot slid its way up his

inner thigh did Hades realise the date was not going to go as planned and it would take everything he had to withstand the assault from Andromeda.

He wanted her - that wasn't in question – and for all intents and purposes, she wanted him, but that was the spell, not her.

"Oh, Haden," she sing-songed over at him, her foot climbing higher still. Only his large palm cupping her ankle stopped it.

"Yes, beautiful," he answered, really trying to see the lighter side of the situation, but that didn't mean he wouldn't punish Cupid later on.

"I'm hungry," she answered, and chewed on her lip. Hades' body responded instantly, making him harder than he had been in a long time.

"What do you want to eat?" he asked, only to have his question answered by her other foot sliding up his thigh.

Removing her feet from his lap, Hades stood and walked around the tale, holding out his hand for Andromeda to take. There would be no conversation out of her until the spell had worn off. Once she was stood, he wrapped his arm around her shoulders and lead her to the exit, nodding to Meton on his way out. The immortal would find his own way home - if he could get away from the small red-head.

"Where are we going?" Andromeda asked, her words slightly slurred as her hands slid over his torso. Hades clenched his teeth, fighting the lust her touch ignited.

"I'm taking you somewhere special," he answered. Maybe, just maybe this would work in his favour. By taking her home - to his home - he could speed up her acceptance of what he was without scaring her. In this state, she would be open to all things otherworldly.

"Oooh, special," she repeated, and giggled, squealing with delight when Hades picked her up in his arms.

"Haden, you smell good," she whispered in his ear. "Haden?" she asked.

"Yes, Andromeda," he answered, only to groan as she licked up his neck and then bit down on his earlobe. He hadn't even realised that area was sensitive until now.

"You taste nice, too."

On swift feet, Hades reached the car, only to skirt around it and head to the back of the building.

Only once he was out of sight did he, along with his squirming cargo, vanish in a flash of light.

Chapter Sixteen

Persephone followed the mortals as they walked down the street. Annoyingly, Hades had decided to take his mortal off somewhere. She had seen them leave the restaurant, but then he had vanished. That meant one thing: he had taken her to the underworld. Persephone soon determined that Hades' disappearance had left the mortal's closest friend and her date alone. If she had learned anything from watching the mortals from Olympus it was that they were sentimental fools and easy to manipulate. Hades' whore would no doubt be extremely keen to see her friend safe and alive.

Blending in with the mortals had been easy. She rather enjoyed it, especially as the males seemed to like her form and the way the clothing clung to her body. She would definitely venture into the world more - after she had taken Olympus - and sample a few of them. With so many variances to choose from, she would be kept busy for a long time. Apollo had taught her a few things that she was most eager to try out.

He had an eclectic taste, and she had learned how to derive the most pleasure from his teachings, but his lessons had become quite boring and, as such, she had sought to learn more from elsewhere. After she had experienced the dark side of love-making, Persephone had craved more. She wanted to go further than a little cutting, play with more than just whips and chains.

Pleasures of the flesh meant so much more to her now, and she would revel in her delights. Persephone grinned as she slowly closed the gap on the two would be lovers, a new idea sparking to life in her brain. The female's companion would be her first mortal tribute from this time, whether he liked it or not. She would just have to get rid of the female sooner rather than later. Persephone would admit that she had dabbled in the pleasures of females, but she preferred men and was quite greedy to have them all to herself. Ideally, the female would have been useful as a bargaining chip, but now she was just in the way.

Calling on her power, Persephone summoned a simple dagger, its razor-sharp edge shimmering in the waning sunlight. Fate, as promised, was on her side as she approached the couple. They had stopped by a small alleyway and were preparing to cross the road. She quickened her own steps and moved up behind the female, whispering so only the male and female could hear her.

"Let's take this party into the alley, shall we?"

"Who the hell are you?" the red head answered angrily, only to gasp then groan as Persephone slid the blade of the dagger through the flesh of her side and up under her ribs. The goddess felt her blood quickly flow down her hand, which only helped to excite her even more.

"Move."

Looking the male in the eyes, she nodded towards the alleyway as the female slumped into her arms, groaning more as Persephone twisted the blade. They had taken only a few steps before the mortal female collapsed. Sighing in disgust, Persephone pushed her into the male's arms, his own face full of regret and sadness as the female touched his cheek and whispered his name before her life left her body, sending her soul to Elyssia.

"Right, now she's out of the way, let's get out of here and have some real fun."

The goddess laughed and called once again on her power. The light enveloped both her and the male, and when that light vanished, so had they, leaving only the cooling body of the female lying on the floor.

The fates had claimed another life thread.

Meton stood and faced the goddess Persephone. He was unsure whether to reveal who he actually was, so instead, he kept quiet. There was no way he would be able to get word to Aphrodite or Hades about what she had just done. Murdering a mortal like she had done was against the law for all Olympians. Not that she followed any rules at all.

Barbara, although scary in her energetic ways, had not deserved to die like she had. She had deserved to find the love of her life and get married. That had all been snatched away, and for what? That was something he didn't know, and from the rumours he had heard about Persephone's hobbies, he didn't want to. He had never been nervous - as a bird, he didn't have much to feel nervous about - but now he was concerned. He had spent so little time in this human form, but he now wanted a chance to master it and court his love. It was blatantly obvious that he was in love with Aphrodite, he always had been. From the time she had visited him as a mortal, he had given her his heart. He had been a dying old man, but she had seen something more and had given him the honour of being her companion.

Now that chance had been lost.

Stood in the centre of her temple, one he had visited many times as an eagle, he waited. She lounged on her throne-like chaise longue dressed in a transparent ochre material that hinted of golds and reds. She was voluptuous and didn't mind showing it off. Only, Meton was not moved by it. In fact, it made his mortal skin crawl knowing why she had brought him here.

"Well, aren't you a pretty one." She leered at him.

Two male servants entered the room, both were what Meton would call, warrior males; packed with muscle and not afraid to get physical. Still new to his form, Meton knew he had little if not no chance of winning against them. He stood still as one held his arms from behind, his grip digging into Meton's skin, as the other took a knife and made quick work of stripping him of all his clothing.

"Oh, yes, such a pretty one." She squealed in delight as she stood and prowled towards him, gesturing for the knife as she approached. Meton swallowed but again said nothing. Her eyes glinted with desire and malice as she trailed the blade from his thigh, up his hip, and across his stomach before she leaned in close, licking his nipple then biting it so hard she drew blood.

Swiping her tongue across her lips, she stood once again.

"Yes, you will do nicely."

Chapter Seventeen

Andromeda was finally where she was meant to be: in his bed. But she was snoring. Hades had been given no choice but to make her sleep off Cupid's love potion. His little mate had become extremely handsy, and he had found it harder and harder to resist her. There was nothing he wanted more than to take her in his arms and show her just how much he wanted her, but he refused to do it like this.

She was a strong, beautiful woman, and he would never take advantage of that. He would rather wait another lifetime for one single touch from her than take advantage. Hades sat in the corner of his chambers, watching her sleep. Her lashes created small shadows on her cheeks, and the tiny snores that came from her pulled at his heartstrings. To him, she was perfection, a blessing from his creator, one that he would cherish and love till he took his last breath.

"My lord," a whispered voice called to him from

the door. One of his servants peeked his head into the room.

"My lord Hades."

"I am here," he answered, and slowly got to his feet.

"You are needed, my lord. The prisoner has asked for you." The servant bowed low.

"I will be right there. Make sure food is brought in case she wakes when I am not here."

"Yes, my lord," the servant replied before he left, closing the door quietly behind him. Hades stood by Andromeda's bedside, his hand snaking out to run the backs of his fingers down her soft cheek. Yes, this felt right, having her here in his home.

Bending his head, Hades kissed her lips gently before he straightened, and with one last look, left the room.

The marble corridors of his chamber felt almost cold. With black being the main colour, would she like his home? Hades mulled it over in his mind as he made his way out of his temple and into his domain.

His guest - or prisoner - Apollo had done nothing but moan continuously since he had been incarcerated. What made Hades laugh - as well as slightly annoy him - was Apollo's continued cries of innocence.

Innocent of what, he had no idea, but the sun god had been placed on the fields of punishment for the time being until Zeus could decide what he wanted to do with him.

It didn't help Hades' patience that Zeus was hardly ever around to deal with something the King of Olympus had a commitment to. In quick strides, Hades walked onto the broken and burnt earth of the fields of punishment. The damned souls scattered, some hissing their dislike and hatred of the god that had trapped them there.

"Ahh, here he is. You took your time," Apollo sneered from his seated position under a broken tree.

"Watch your tongue, Apollo," Hades ordered. He was in no mood to be dealing with a god who had a superiority complex. "What is it that you want?" he asked, not bothering with any niceties.

The golden god slowly got to his feet and walked towards Hades. His face covered in dirt and soot, he wasn't the pristine powerful being he acted.

"You need to watch out for Persephone," he said simply.

"And why is that, why should I listen to you? You have done more harm than good," Hades fired back, and turned to walk away. If this was all Apollo had to say, he would leave. He was already aware that the goddess was missing a few screws, but there was little she could do to hurt him.

"Just watch out for her," Apollo called out after him. "Her soul is black."

Hades stopped and looked back over his shoulder at the god. A feeling of dread settled uneasily in his stomach, and he faced his temple. Instead of walking back, he vanished and reappeared in his chamber.

Andromeda was no longer sleeping. She was gone.

Andromeda looked out over the balcony of the bedroom she had been asleep in. The room itself was magnificent; black and white marble surrounded her and she loved it. Every luxury was present, along with an obscene number of gemstones. They were the first thing she had noticed. They had been included in every piece of decoration, but instead of looking wrong and overdone, it suited the room.

She had awoken from a strange dream, one filled with images she had seen before, but this time, instead of not making sense, they played like a story board. Whatever had been in the garlic bread that she had eaten when she had sat down for the date with

Haden had done more than make her feel a combination of drunk and high.

Her date was another subject entirely. She now knew who he was, and what he was, and she was still processing how she felt about that. But the dream, visions - whatever you wanted to describe them as - were still playing over and over in her mind.

She now understood why she felt attracted to Haden, and why she felt like she had seen him before. Andromeda understood more than ever now; that this was not her first life. Everything that had happened both in this life and the previous one, made sense. They were leading her to something more important than her stupid ex-boyfriend and jewellery shop. Whilst she was annoyed that she had been slipped something that made her act like a total fool, she was thankful because most would probably be freaking out.

Now, as she looked at the view, she felt confused yet also at home. Everything seemed familiar; the sky that was dotted with diamonds, showing every constellation, the beautiful meadows that stretched to the horizon and beyond, and the dark, burnt pit of hell that ran alongside the meadows. This was home, it was that simple. Her heart felt settled as she looked over the scene and focused on the long, lazy river that bisected the meadows. She knew what that was, but unlike before, she didn't feel compelled to visit.

She didn't need to.

"Andromeda," a deep voice called out, and she closed her eyes. When she had awoken and he wasn't there, she had been disappointed, but now she was just glad to hear his voice and see him again. The date was a fussy mess of images in her mind, especially after she had eaten the garlic bread. But she did remember feeling less shy and more inclined to feeling Haden up.

Haden. She smiled and shook her head. Everything had already started to click into place in her mind, and she could now deal with the rest that didn't make sense. Or did it?

Andromeda turned and faced him as he walked out onto the balcony, still dressed in the clothes he wore for the date. He looked just as gorgeous now as he had been then.

"Hi," she answered shyly, but her heart had already set off at a well-timed trot.

"Everything ok?" he asked nervously, stepping closer. "I was worried when I didn't see you resting. How's your head?"

"Yeah, it's ok, a little fuzzy." She smiled and turned again to look at the view. "So…" she said, and waited for him to join her at the rail, feeling comfortable as he copied her position, elbows leaning on the marble.

"So…" he repeated.

"I'm taking it your name isn't Haden, then," she started.

"No, it's not," he answered, and dropped his head. She watched his shoulders heave as a loud sigh left him.

"Hey," Andromeda soothed, resting one hand on his back and the other on one of his incredibly large biceps. She waited until he had turned his head to look at her. His eyes were mesmerising, and now she knew why they felt so familiar.

"It's ok, you know," she said.

"It's ok?" he questioned, and she nodded.

"It's ok that you didn't tell me who you are. I reckon most women would think you were nuts."

"And you don't think I'm nuts?" he asked as he pushed off the railing and stood to his full height, causing her to crane her neck in order to look at him.

"No," was all she could say, as once again their eyes' locked. How did he do this to her every time?

She didn't flinch when his large hands cupped her cheek, his eyes releasing their hold as they searched her face. "You know who - what - I am?"

Andromeda nodded. Her chest felt as heavy as the atmosphere that had grown thick with tension.

"Say it, Andromeda. If you know my name, let me hear it from your lips," he said, only an inch or so separating their mouths.

"Hades," she breathed. "Lord of the dead."

"And this doesn't scare you?" he asked as he pressed light, gentle kisses to her cheek, moving over her nose to the other cheek. "Doesn't bother you, that I am a god?"

"No," she answered, and that was how she honestly felt. If she searched deep inside her heart, she had known all along, and in her heart, she had loved him all along as well. He was the man from every single dream. He was the one she yearned to run to. Her soul called out to him like no other, and only with him could she ever find peace. Every time she had died, she had never regretted it, for she would see Hades again.

Only this time, she wasn't dead.

"No, it doesn't scare me," she admitted again as she looked at his handsome face. She beheld his look of wariness, almost like he didn't quite trust what he was hearing.

"You should be," he said. "I am not worthy of you."

Andromeda felt the hurt in his voice deep down in her core, where her soul, connected to her body, ached with the need to help Hades.

Did she have the courage to take another small step and admit out loud, for all to hear, what she felt? Yes, she had only really met him the other day - they barely knew anything about each other that wasn't rumour or hearsay - but her heart led the way now. Hades was her future.

"You are worthy," she whispered. "Worthy of my love."

Chapter Eighteen

"You love me?" Hades asked. He didn't hide the shock in his voice. His eyes were wide and, if only for a second, mirrored that of an innocent boy.

"Yes, I love you. I always have. In every single life I have lived." To most people, that sentence would have had her well on her way to donning a straitjacket and earning her a bed at the nut farm, but with Hades, everything was different. The rules had changed.

She realised now that the dreams that had plagued her most of her life were, in fact, memories, snippets of the lives she had lived, and her deaths. They showed her every single time she had entered this realm and every single time she had met the lord of the underworld. It was only now she could see the pain each meeting had cost him.

Each and every time she had entered his domain

it had been like a knife to his chest, knowing his soulmate was there yet not able to be together.

Andromeda knew, without a doubt, that she loved him. She felt it in her very soul, and now she had accepted it. It would take a lot more than gods and fate to stop her finally getting the happily ever after she felt she deserved.

A frown marred Hades' forehead, his eyes unfocussed as he looked at nothing. "I thought…" he started, only to stop mid-sentence, his face scrunched as he seemed to struggle to think.

"You thought what?" Andromeda asked, placing her hands over his, where he had left them on her cheeks.

"I thought I would have to do more - fight more - that it wouldn't be this easy."

Andromeda smiled and stroked the back of his hands.

"Haven't you fought enough?" she asked in return, and when he didn't answer, she continued, "Why shouldn't it be easy, Hades?" Andromeda loved the way his name - his real name - flowed from her lips.

Easy, unforced, meant to be.

"Love shouldn't have to be hard, it shouldn't be difficult." She watched as he frowned, her words slowly sinking in. She could tell it would take a lot more to convince him. Moving forward, Andromeda rose onto her tiptoes and kissed him gently on the cheek, enjoying the way his stubble tickled her skin.

"I know most think it has to be hard to be worth it, but haven't we been through enough?" she asked, her own mind drifting back to the many memories. "Haven't *you* been through enough?"

Their eyes met and Andromeda was faced with a magnitude of emotion as Hades fought back tears.

His voice was a croak as he moved his hands from her face and instead wrapped his arms around her waist, pulling her into his body. "I've waited so long for you, watched from the shadows as time and time again you were taken from me." He pressed his forehead to hers. "I couldn't protect you."

Andromeda's heart swelled with love for this man, for behind everything - the immortal, the god, the ruler of the underworld - he was still, in essence, a man.

And he, just like any other in the world, deserved the chance to be loved.

Hades had no words, his brain only focused on one

single thing: she loved him. That was all he needed. Pulling her even closer to his body, Hades held her tight with one arm whilst the other snaked up Andromeda's back. He fingered her braid before wrapping it around his fist and tugging gently, until her head tilted. His eyes searched hers for any sign of doubt, fear, or unwillingness, but instead only saw love and acceptance.

With gentle touches, Hades pressed his lips to hers. Unlike the kiss in the bar, this was a kiss *he* dominated. He stroked her lips, savouring her flavour, her softness, before he licked across the seam, demanding entrance. Her breathy moan urged him to deepen their duel, his tongue battling with hers. Andromeda's hands against his chest, pressed then clawed, almost like a cat, showing him in action that she also felt the need he did. The need to be close, to touch, to get lost in their passion. Hades had waited centuries for this - for her, his mate, his love, to be in his arms.

"Andromeda," he whispered as their mouths separated and Hades started a path across her cheek and down her neck. He was addicted. For a being that had been deprived of touch and emotion for so long, he wasn't sure he would be able to stop.

Her breaths were laboured in his ear, and Hades

revelled at the sound, knowing it was because of him. Moving his hands once again, he slid both down her back, tracing every curve and indent, his fingers skating over each vertebra and receiving an answering shiver in return. His large hands finished their descent over her buttocks. Cupping the globes of flesh, he pulled her against him as he continued to lick and suck Andromeda's neck.

He felt her hands release his t-shirt from their tight grip before they travelled up and around his neck. He wanted - needed - her closer. Earning a small squeal, Hades picked Andromeda up by the buttocks, bringing her heated core in direct contact with his own hard arousal. Their moans mingled in unison as Hades moved his mouth back to dominate Andromeda's. Her taste was addictive, there was no way he would ever tire of it, not in this lifetime or the next.

Hades rested Andromeda on the top of the marble railing, but didn't release her. Now he had her in his arms, it would take a lot to get him to let go. Slowing the kiss, reluctantly, Hades pulled away to rest his forehead against her own. Their breaths and heartbeats mirrored one another's.

"Wow, that's some kiss," she whispered, her

fingers stroking the back of his neck and under his hair line. A touch that caused him to shiver.

"Wow indeed," he repeated, and squeezed her to him. This was a far too important moment for them both to rush. He needed to know that if they continued, it was something she wanted just as badly as he did.

And he was nervous. The big, bad lord and god of the underworld was nervous about having sex with a mortal. His brothers would laugh. But this wasn't just a fling with a nymph or random mortal that he would discard afterwards. This was the keeper of his heart. Their first steps together would not be ruined by haste.

"Andromeda…" he started, only to feel fingertips against his lips, stopping him.

"Shush. Why are you overthinking things?" she asked, and slowly slid her fingers away from his mouth, replacing them with her lips for a quick kiss.

"I can see it in your eyes," she continued. "The look of worry, uncertainty." Her hands traced his face, smoothing over the frown lines he knew were present.

"I just want you to be sure," Hades explained. "Sure that you want me and all the crap that comes with it. This isn't a one-off, Andromeda. You accept me now, and it's for always, because there is no way, on your world or my own, that I will ever be letting you go."

His declaration almost felt like official vows, and he would treat them as such. Hades was no Zeus; he would never be untrue and would love Andromeda until his last breath. Of that he didn't need the fates' confirmation; he knew it in his soul.

"Say yes, Andromeda. Be mine forever, like I am yours."

Chapter Nineteen

Andromeda struggled to draw a deep enough breath to calm her nerves. She felt on the edge of an anxiety attack, but she wasn't anxious. In fact, she felt invigorated, more alive than she had felt in a long time, and it was all down to the incredibly handsome man in front of her.

With her mother bringing her up like she had, Andromeda had always had an open mind to things that most people thought was out of the norm. So, declaring herself to a man that she had only ever met twice - in this life time – didn't feel wrong to her. In a short space of time, she had realised that fate worked in strange ways for a reason.

It had all become so clear after she had woken up from her out of character nap. Andromeda didn't know what had been in the garlic bread, but whatever it had been, it had opened her eyes and made her, in essence, see the light.

See that life was far too short to not follow your heart.

As she looked into Hades' deep, dark eyes, Andromeda saw only love reflected back at her, something she had never seen with her ex. Hades had loved her through the centuries, not minding what she looked like. He loved her soul, and that meant more to her than any romantic words or gestures.

"Hades," she whispered back, and smiled, "I've been yours since we first met."

His answering smile made Andromeda's legs weak, but she had little time to dwell on it as his lips once again took control of an earth-shattering kiss that swept her away on a tide of emotion and passion. As his tongue delved into her mouth, Andromeda relinquished every wall she had built, let go of the hurt that had been done to her heart and embraced what Hades had to give.

His growl deepened as Andromeda sucked his tongue into her mouth. She felt his fingers tighten on her buttocks as he pulled her against him, his hard length pressing against her clit. The pleasure of this simple move washed over her. Dragging her legs up, she wrapped them around his waist, locking her ankles and rotated her hips so on every downstroke, his hardness caressed her.

"Fuck." He growled again before lifting her off the railing. His lips took over the kiss as he slowly walked them back into his bedroom. Andromeda wouldn't have cared if they had stayed out on the balcony, she was lost in the feel of his lips on hers.

The lights of the bedroom had been dimmed since she was last in the room, but Andromeda could still make out every feature on Hades' face; the way his nose slanted, the shape of his lips, the heat and desire that filled his gaze as he gently laid her down on the large bed.

The softness of the fur and silk sheets welcomed her into their embrace as Hades released her to lie by her side, his head propped up on his hand with his other stroking every free bit of skin available. She had been forced to unlock her ankles from around his waist and she now missed the weight of him. Instead of rushing into stripping her, as expected, Hades surprised her by taking his sweet time. He would start with her buttons - the ones on her shirt and jeans - popping one and then seeking a kiss.

He continued this pace, driving Andromeda wild, making her sit and remove one sleeve, then the next, before pushing the straps of her bra down. In no time at all, she lay on the bedcovers, completely naked and breathless from his gentle touches.

Andromeda arched into his hands as he cupped her breasts, teasing the nipples to hard peaks with his thumbs, her own hands fisting the sheets below her. When she opened her eyes to meet his, she gasped at the desire she saw, his deep blue orbs glittering with barely supressed lust.

"You are so beautiful," he growled out as he leaned over her, sucking a nipple into his mouth. His tongue flicked the tight bud, causing an answering pulse in her pussy. His large hand held her stomach, his grip not punishingly tight but firm enough that she knew she couldn't move under his onslaught.

She felt his own arousal as he thrust against her thigh, his mouth moving its attention to her other nipple, giving it the same attention as the first. Andromeda was a slave to his touch, wave after wave of pleasure coursed through her, making her head fuzzy and her limbs weak.

The hand that had held her down moved lower, his fingers trailing a scorching path as he aimed for her core. She was soaked, of that she was certain. Her pussy had been wet the moment his lips had met hers. As his fingers found her bundle of nerves, she gasped. Her clit had become hyper-sensitive and reacted to even the lightest of touches.

When his searching fingers found her entrance,

he growled low, causing another gush of pleasure to fall from her.

"Fuck, so wet." His voice was coarse and low as he gently inserted one finger, his thumb circling her clit. Releasing one hand from the bed sheets, Andromeda searched for Hades, and when she found his stomach, she quickly moved her arm down until she found his hard length, hidden from her by his jeans. She groaned as she felt its length and girth, her pussy clenching around his finger at the thought of it entering her and sending her to heights she had only ever dreamed of.

"Hades," she groaned, and pushed her hips into his touch, moaning encouragement as he pushed another - then another - finger into her hot core. His thumb circled her clit faster and faster as he pumped his hand, bringing her pleasure she had only about read in books.

"Andromeda," he growled again as his lips once more found hers. He pushed his tongue into her mouth, dominating it as he found a quick pace with his fingers, bringing her to the precipice.

"Give it to me, Andromeda. Give it all to me," he panted as he pushed his fingers deep inside her core - pressing a button she never knew she had - and pinched her clit. Her back bowed off the bed as pleasure – never-ending pleasure - ripped through her. Sparks ignited behind her eyes and she screamed, not caring if anyone would hear. Her orgasm seemed to go on and on as Hades forced every ounce of ecstasy out of her, not letting her rest until her body twitched with sensitivity.

Hades watched as Andromeda's body shattered in pleasure, reacting in the most delicious way to his continuous onslaught. Her body sensitive to his each and every touch, he had quickly learned what took her up and then what brought her back down. Simple things that would allow making love to her last longer and have her screaming his name.

Hades wanted all of her pleasure, and the most arrogant side of him wanted to wipe the memory of every male she had been with before him, make her only remember his touch and how he had made her feel.

The sounds she made as he took her nipples in his mouth had nearly undone him. He had thrust against her leg, desperate to feel her heat surround him. He had been thirsting to see her release, to watch her erupt with pleasure. And that she had done - and more.

Hades had nearly released inside his jeans as she had screamed out and squeezed her dainty hand around his cock.

Hades looked down at Andromeda's flushed body and grinned. Here was his mate, at his mercy. He once again leaned down to take her lips in a punishing kiss. His repeated growl of, "Mine," were answered with a shiver from his mate. As his fingers slowly slipped from her soaked core and he released her lips, he held her attention by licking those fingers clean.

"Definitely mine," he rumbled, and moved off the bed, pinning her with his gaze when Andromeda went to sit up. "Stay, don't move."

Standing at the edge of the bed, he spent a moment looking down at her. Her pale hair had come loose from its braid and flowed around her, her skin was flushed a beautiful pale pink, and her eyes, glazed with pleasure, looked up at him.

"By Olympus you are stunning." His voice nearly broke at the emotions rolling through him. Slowly, he peeled his t-shirt from his body, enjoying the way Andromeda's eyes widened as his torso came into view.

Hades had never been shy of the way he looked, he was graced, like his brothers, with good looks - of that he knew - but the way Andromeda gazed at him now made him feel like the most powerful man in the world.

Sliding his hands down his chest and abdomen, loving the way her eyes followed every movement, he flicked the top button of his jeans open and was rewarded by her tongue gliding out to lick her lips.

His cock jumped in response.

Sliding the zip down slowly, he kept his eyes on hers, loving every little reaction. Hades was as hard as marble by the time he pushed his jeans down over his hips. When the girls had shown him what mortals wore, he had avoided the underwear they had insisted he needed. He refused to encase his manhood in the tight material for fear they would cut off the blood circulation. Instead, he wore nothing, and from Andromeda's reaction, she liked it, too.

His hard cock sprang free, its tip swollen and already tipped with precum as he kicked off his boots and the jeans. Using his hands, he parted Andromeda's legs and crawled between them, rubbing the soft skin as he did so.

"So soft," he whispered. "So wet," he added as his hand found her core, checking she was ready for him. He moved his other hand to his cock, pumping it up and down. The friction felt good, but not as good as being inside his mate. He smiled, feeling smug as Andromeda refused to take her eyes from where his hand stroked himself.

"You want this?" he asked as two fingers pushed inside her. Her body reacted and clamped down on him. She nodded in response, but it wasn't enough.

He pressed his thumb once again to her clit and repeated, "Do you want this, Andromeda? Do you want my hard cock inside you? Tell me or else you won't get it," he demanded.

"Yes," she answered, albeit quietly. "I want it, Hades," she paused as he flicked her clit, "please."

Removing his fingers, he moved to lean over her body, brushing his lips across her own as he aligned the swollen head of his cock with her entrance, and pushed in an inch.

"Anything for you," he breathed, and pushed in another inch. "Anything for my soulmate." He groaned as he pushed again, seating himself fully, her body accepting his as his balls rested against her arse.

Elyssia, that's what this felt like, his own personal Elyssia. She fit him like she was made for him and him alone.

"Fuck," he growled out as Andromeda moved her legs to wrap around his waist, forcing him deeper still.

"Oh, gods," she moaned, her core clenching around him, and he was lost.

"Hold on tight, Andromeda," he breathed. "This may get a little rough." And Hades let loose all the desire and frustration he had built up over the centuries. This night, they wouldn't be able to tell where one finished and the other began. There would be no doubt come morning who Andromeda belonged to as Hades finally claimed his mate.

Chapter Twenty

Meton was blinded by intense pain. It had only been a short while since Persephone had finally left him alone yet there wasn't an area of his body that didn't hurt. It had been centuries since he'd had a body to worry about, and he was positive the spell that had been cast upon him would finally end, and as such, send him back to being an eagle.

He needed to get back to Olympus. When the excruciating pain and thoughts of wings and his goddess swirled through his mind, the goddess who had captured him had sliced his skin, rubbing her body in his blood and trying to get him sexually aroused as she spoke over and over of what she would do when she ruled over all the gods.

Her plans sickened him - she sickened him - and it was only the thoughts of his goddess that had gotten him through his ordeal so far. Her face came easily to mind - that and her kind smile, beautiful eyes, and wicked laugh.

Aphrodite would always be his goddess. She would always have his heart.

"Awwww, poor Meton, are you missing your mistress?" Persephone's sickly-sweet voice called from the doorway. She sauntered into the room wearing nothing, his blood still coating her skin. How she had found out who he was, he didn't know, but it wouldn't bode well for him or his future. Staying silent, Meton tugged on the chains that tied him to a large metal-framed bed, they scraped across the surface, making Meton wince, the sound almost like fingernails on slate.

"Oh dear, are you still not talking to me? Oh well." She smiled and ran a nail up his torso then back down again before she scraped it across the length of his cock. Meton bit his lip. Whenever she touched him, he was repulsed, and if he had anything left in his stomach, he would have vomited it up long ago.

Persephone slowly knelt on the bed before she straddled his naked form, placing her core over his cock and rubbing it seductively.

"You will respond to me," she stated, then leaned

forward, taking his earlobe in her teeth and biting hard. "But your mistress will never find you. You will be mine forever, to do with as I please." She licked where she had bitten before she sat back, wiggling more.

"And please me you will, Meton. Whether you want to or not."

Hades paced the long length of the main room in Zeus's temple. Why his brother needed such a large room was beyond him. Maybe the power had gone to his head, like the rumours had said. In all honesty, he couldn't give a shit. Right now, he wanted to be in one place and one place only, and Zeus's temple was not it. His mate was currently sleeping off an exhausting night of love-making, and here he was, waiting for his brother to show up. It annoyed the shit out of him that he had been summoned yet his brother couldn't actually be arsed to receive him. Hades hadn't seen Zeus for at least a few months, not since he went off with the elder Oracle to discuss whatever they discussed. Zeus never saw fit to unveil his plans to anyone, even if it affected them.

"Brother."

"Finally," Hades mumbled under his breath. "You summoned me. What's wrong?"

"Nothing's wrong. Can't I ask to see my own brother?" Zeus smiled but Hades could tell it was forced.

"I call bullshit on that. Not once have you ever just summoned me because you wanted to 'see your brother'."

Hades felt on edge. Every moment away from Andromeda made him more and more afraid she would be gone when he returned. Finally, after such a long time, he had felt complete and whole. With her in his arms and by his side, he could deal with anything.

"Am I that transparent?"

Hades just glared at Zeus. "Or just plain stupid for thinking I am that clueless."

"Point taken." Zeus paused then continued, each word released heated Hades' blood.

"I know about the mortal in your bed, Hades. You cannot, and will not, keep her."

"What?"

"You know your fate."

"How about you fuck off, brother. Who I have in

my bed is none of your business. I don't make comments about the whores you keep company with. I don't tell you you can't do this or do that. On what earth do you think you have the right?"

"I am lord and god of Olympus, Hades. Or did you forget?"

"How can I when you trumpet it about. How about you remember who helped you get there, brother." Hades sneered the word. "You forget it was all three of us that defeated father, not just you. You have been so wrapped up in your own self-importance you've forgotten the facts. How about getting your head out of your arse long enough to see that the world does not, in fact, revolve around you anymore."

He paused before continuing, "We are obsolete in the mortal world now. No one worships us, no one believes. How about you deal with that instead of worrying about who I am fucking."

Hades' blood had reached boiling point. He had never argued with his siblings, but Zeus had stepped over a line. He would never tell any of the gods what they couldn't or shouldn't do. But then again, all Hades wanted to do was go back to the underworld and forget everyone else other than his mate and the charges under his protection.

"I remember, Hades, but I also remember you agreeing to do whatever it took to be lord of the underworld. I also remember what the fates said."

Hades continued to glare at Zeus

"I don't bow down to the sisters, Zeus. Their dark magic and warped minds have no place in our world. Just like us, they are an outdated tradition," Hades argued.

"The sisters decide our fates, they always have and always will."

"They don't decide mine," Hades countered, his fists clenching.

With sad eyes, Zeus replied, "You cannot defy fate, Hades."

Hades lifted his chin, defiance now pulsing through his bloodstream. Turning, he walked towards the door before he looked at Zeus over his shoulder. His words, although said quietly, echoed throughout the temple.

"Just fucking watch me." He paused at the door, almost waiting to see if Zeus would answer. When only silence came, Hades left. Instead of heading back to his domain and to the woman that occupied every thought, he moved off towards the entrance to earth herself. He would deal with fate once and for all.

Their archaic traditions and grasp on power had no place in the modern world, and they would not dictate his future.

His future was his to decide, and it would be with his mate.

Chapter Twenty-One

Aphrodite sipped the steaming cup of coffee in her hand as she sat in her new favourite coffee shop and watched the world go by. Worry caused her usually carefree face to frown as she looked out onto the street, but she didn't see the people walk by, or the cars as they rushed past.

She wasn't worried about Hades, she was pleased with how his courting was going and hadn't been at all surprised when she had found out he had taken Andromeda back to the underworld. All she hoped was that the female would have an open mind and maybe open her heart. Aphrodite knew the female had been having regular dreams that concerned her past lives. It had been the only way, without interfering completely, that Aphrodite could help prepare her. No, there was a lot more at stake than Hades getting laid, as Sonia would have said. The balance of the immortals themselves was wavering. Hades needed the energy that came from pairing with his soulmate for the balance to be reset. What Apollo had started as a revenge scheme had upset things to the point Olympus itself was in danger.

Zeus had already been made aware, but none of the other gods had figured it out, so Aphrodite was doing what she could before a full-scale panic happened. Yes, they were gods, but some of them would run around, hands in the air, screaming.

What had her more than worried was the lack of communication from Meton. Since he had left for the joint date with Hades, she had heard nothing from him. Not that she expected him to contact her all the time, but she did expect something.

A part of her - a huge part of her - was jealous that another woman was getting to spend time with him, and do it whilst he was in the human form. It had been centuries since she had seen him in any form but an eagle, and when she had first seen him, he had been near the end of his life, succumbing to old age. But to see him like she had, at his prime, her heart had nearly stopped.

He was gorgeous. But he didn't belong to her, so if he had gone off with the mortal's friend then she wouldn't have blamed him at all. He had been an eagle for a long time, so wanting to experience the pleasure of being a human again was to be expected.

She may have accepted it in her head, but her heart hurt, her chest felt sore and heavy. Something was wrong, she could feel it in the energies. Her gut-feeling was confirmed when Hermes rushed through the coffee shop doors. Dressed as a mortal, like Aphrodite, he looked around until he finally met her gaze. He quickly made it to her side and sat down. Worry, like what was marring her face, marred his.

"Goddess," he said quietly, "Meton is missing."

Those three words caused her heart to stop and her stomach to flip.

"What?" she asked, and fought back the fear that threatened to engulf her.

"He left the restaurant with the mortal female not long after Hades left with his mate," Hermes started to explain. "They had to leave early because Andromeda had become a little hard to deal with."

Aphrodite frowned. "Hard to deal with? She's a mortal."

Hermes winced a little. "Cupid slipped her something in her food. Safe to say, Hades had to take her back to the underworld for her to sleep it off."

"He did what?" she exclaimed, causing the other patrons of the coffee house to look at her. "I swear I am going to..." Aphrodite started, but then stopped and sighed. "I need to talk to Psyche about him, he's getting worse again."

"Yes, goddess," Hermes replied. "Meton left with the mortal female. He had offered to walk her home before he himself returned to Olympus. I watched them leave and then left myself, only he never arrived and I can't find him on my map." Hermes seemed more than annoyed that his mystical map, that showed the location of every god, goddess, and companion, was failing in this particular task. It was his gift; he could deliver a message to anyone of them, anywhere.

"It's like he's vanished completely." Hermes sighed.

"What about the mortal female?" Aphrodite questioned. "Have you asked her?"

"My lady," Hermes started, "the mortal female was found dead only five minutes' walk from the restaurant. She had been stabbed in the heart and left in an alley. There was no sign of Meton."

Aphrodite was stunned. Meton would never have killed anyone, it just wasn't in his nature.

"He didn't do it, Hermes, that isn't Meton," she said. The doubt on Hermes' face said he didn't quite believe it.

"My lady, the energies there were from an immortal, and he was the last one to be seen with her."

Hermes took one of her hands into his own and stroked the soft skin. "I'm sorry, my lady."

Aphrodite shook her head. Denial lacing her voice, she snapped, "No! No, he didn't do it."

She took a deep breath and continued more calmly, yet the demand in her tone was still easily found, "Find him, Hermes, because something doesn't feel right." She swallowed and forced back the tears.

"We return home," she said, and ignored the mortals as she vanished in a blinding flash of light.

Chapter Twenty-Two

Hades stood at the entrance to the path that lead down into the bowels of the earth, anger still boiling in his blood from what Zeus had said. A part of him, deep down, knew and understood where he was coming from, but this was his life, his existence, and it was his to live. Zeus had his mate, although the way they treated each other was bang out of order. With Andromeda in his life now, there was nothing he wouldn't do to keep her by his side. She made his world tolerable. There had been a time when each day was becoming more and more difficult to deal with, but with her, now each day held the promise of love and happiness.

The air that flowed from the tunnel smelled damp and old, and a hint of aging decay hit his senses. Most would have turned back, fled from the possibility of dealing with the three sisters. Those that did have the courage often met with a grizzly end.

Along with being immortal, the sisters had a vengeful sense of humour. Nothing they did came without a cost, and they had a particular taste for human flesh. Hades blamed his own father and the titans for the way they were. Locked away, only useful for their gift of telling the future, they had to survive on what they had.

But they had grown too powerful and demanded much. Yes, when he had taken the task of watching over the underworld, he had done it because of those three. Death had not been a release, it had been a permanent purgatory for anyone who passed. He had taken on every task set before him, but now he would not stand for their involvement. Fate was not theirs to dictate. He refused to allow them to force their will.

Still dressed in his modern clothing, Hades walked down the tunnel, his steps echoing loudly against the rock walls. He knew his presence would have already been expected. They had the foresight, of course, but what he didn't want them to know were his plans.

He stepped into a cavern that reminded him of the old entrance to the underworld that they had resided in many centuries before. Pools of oil that had been lit were littered across the floor. Bones from both animal and human lay in heaps from where they had fallen. The floor was damp, and it wasn't from water. Dirt, blood, and flesh, among other things, made Hades' stomach turn.

The air was heavy with death, but Hades was not afraid.

"Hades, you honour us," their crackled voices called out from their bed of decaying furs that took up an entire wall. Their barely-clad bodies writhed, a collection of arms and legs, skin and bone.

"We know why you have come. We know all." Their voices, as one, rose and fell with pitch, and Hades stepped forward.

"We know about your mate. Fate cannot be changed. Hers was set in motion when you took on your powers. and it cannot be stopped."

One sister disentangled herself from the writhing forms of the others and climbed off the bed. Her body was encased only in a sheer shroud that left nothing to the imagination. Only her body was no longer toned and firm but old and decaying.

"Your mate is destined to live but die young. Her circle of life cannot be changed no matter how much you want it, Hades. Her soul will be reborn, as it should, but you will never get to keep her."

Hades didn't move as the sister circled him. Her words cut at his heart. He would try with everything he had to keep Andromeda with him. If he had to break the wheel and end the cycle, so be it. He attempted to repress a shudder as he felt a hand on his back, but the touch sent chills down his spine.

"Pity you are so focused on this mate of yours, we could make you quite happy, Lord Hades."

Her words where whispered, but still Hades felt like his stomach would rebel.

"No. As I said… Pity." She finished her circling and stood in front of him, a mocking smile upon her face. Hades' blood began its slow boil once again.

"Your Andromeda will die," she stated, and tilted her head, her sneer doing nothing to calm the rage that wanted to take over. "And you will be powerless to stop it."

Still he said nothing.

"We are the fates," they chorused as one. The sister that stood raised her hands into the air and lifted her face.

"We are the power, we are true rulers of this earth. All humans and gods will die."

The single green eye in her head, pinned him with its glare. "Even you will die, we have seen it."

Finally, Hades spoke, "No, you only see what you want to happen, only what will give you the most power."

Reaching out quickly, his large hand wrapped around the throat of the closest sister, cutting off her words. Her claws fought his grip in an attempt to get him to release her.

"You are not power. You are not the rulers of this world or the next." His own power flowed through him, making the fires around the cavern grow, their heat burning away the putrid, decaying flesh that had been left to fester.

"You may be the fates, but you do not dictate mine or anyone else's future."

His words filled the chamber, echoing off the rock as his power rose.

"You will lose, Hades. Her life has already been forfeit," the sister spat out as he refused to release his hand on her throat. Her warning made his heart stutter. He had left Andromeda alone for too long.

"You have no power anymore," he announced, and released his power.

Screams replaced their spiteful words as his fire, summoned from the centre of the earth, engulfed the sisters, wrapping them in its glowing embrace, burning away their bodies until only bone remained, then turning even those to ash.

Hades stood in the cavern of the fates, unburned, as what remained of their power drifted away on a breeze. He had done what he should have done years before. Hades turned and moved back up the tunnel. His gut and heart told him to get back to his realm, to his mate. The fates' last warning echoed in his skull and pushed him to move faster.

Andromeda stretched her arms over her head and grinned, her body felt deliciously sore everywhere. Every muscle ached from use, especially between her legs. She would be feeling the effects of Hades' loving for days, and that was her main reason for grinning. He had taken no prisoners the night before, and had even marked every inch of her skin with his lips. She knew there would most likely be bruises from where he had held her wrists and hands to keep her from touching him. He had taken complete control of her body, and she had loved every second of it.

With each memory her body flushed and tingled, and if Hades had been next to her, she would have crawled her way up his body to taste every inch of it. Not only did they do the dirty into the small hours of the morning, but they talked.

Conversed like they had known each other forever, and that was honestly how she felt about

Hades. The big, brooding god of the history books wasn't brooding at all. Yes, he was big and muscled and sexy, but never brooding. He had admitted himself that he had simply been lonely, and then after finally finding the soul for him, only to see it reincarnate time after time, he became disheartened about ever finding his soulmate.

There had been a time in Andromeda's life when the idea of a soulmate and love was a joke. That was after Russell had made her feel like she didn't deserve it. Yet, here was a man who would literally give her the world, or underworld, for that matter.

Sliding out of bed, Andromeda pulled on a dark blue robe that Hades had left out for her. There was fruits and wine on the table as well, but she wasn't hungry. She walked back out to the balcony and again looked at the view; the home of the dead. Hades had left her an hour before, kissing her sweetly and grabbing her arse. Andromeda laughed to herself, Hades seemed to have an unhealthy obsession with her arse. But she didn't mind. Not at all. In fact, she had pouted when he had left to go do 'god business', but he had said he wouldn't be long.

A loud whimpering pulled Andromeda's attention from the view before her. The sound resonated in her heart; someone or something was in pain and scared.

On her feet, she followed the sound as best she could, barely making a noise on the marble steps.

The stairs lead to a private garden, filled with trees and statues. Midnight flowers like moonflowers, night phlox, and datura's filled the beds, their scents reaching her in the gentle breeze. The garden had a magical feel, and Andromeda felt completely at home. Her hand drifted over the flowers as she passed, loving the feel of the silk petals on her skin as she followed the whimpering that continued to rise in volume. She passed a small stream, whose waters glittered like it had been filled with diamonds.

The feeling Andromeda had was similar to what Alice must have felt like when she entered Wonderland. Awe and excitement seeped into her very bones. As she stepped over the stream, Andromeda noticed the whimpering had turned to gentle howls. The sound filled with sorrow, it pulled her in. She quickened her pace, passing through a large gate, where her feet froze. In front of her was a very, very large, three-headed dog.

But unlike the history books, he wasn't growling and snarling or showing his fangs. He lay, whimpering and howling as he licked his paw, his eyes sad. And Andromeda fell in love.

She had always been an animal person, but with

Russell, she was not allowed any pets, and when she had gotten back on her own feet, she just didn't have the time to take care of one. But now, looking at this beautiful creature, she was lost.

Approaching slowly, she called out his name - anyone who knew anything about Greek mythology would know who Cerberus was. Hell hound of the underworld and puppy-dog of the dead if the looks of him were anything to go by.

"Shush," she whispered soothingly, and was met by the saddest face she had ever seen. Cerberus was, in essence, a giant dogue de bordeaux, stacked with muscle, and fangs that could cut through muscle and bone, and yet, a face that could melt hearts. His eyes - all six of them - were a dark chocolate-brown and looked so sad, Andromeda could feel the hurt emanating from him.

"It's ok, sweetie," she continued, smiling sweetly as he growled low and pulled his paw back under him.

"Cerberus," she called out a little firmer, showing him she was in charge. "Let me see it."

As she approached, Cerberus tried to back away, but he was already too large for his pen and had nowhere to go. "Oh, sweetie," she cried as she saw a large open gash on his left paw.

Slowly lowering herself onto her knees, Andromeda reached out and stroked one of his heads, his noses inches from where she sat. She gently stroked his fur, letting him get used to her scent, and before long they were sniffing her and letting her close enough to look at his injured paw. Luckily, it was shallow and wouldn't need any tending to other than keeping clean. But he was doing that fine on his own.

Cerberus was as Andromeda first thought; a big puppy-dog that loved attention. After five minutes he had come out of his small hut and was as close as he could possibly be without crushing her. His long tail smacked against the earth, creating a loud beating sound that accompanied little huffs and whines as he begged for more attention.

"Aww, you are such a good boy." She laughed as one of his heads licked her cheek, her mind so focused on the big puppy she missed the presence of someone else.

"Andromeda?"

Chapter Twenty-Three

Persephone had watched Hades' little tart as she stepped onto the balcony. It still amazed her -and pissed her off - that one of the elder gods would settle for pathetic mortal. They were no use for anything – well, unless they had good stamina and big cocks. She grinned, her current entertainment was chained to a wall in her temple and was showing surprising resilience to her games. A shiver skated its way down her back as she remembered the pleasure. He may not last much longer, but by that point she would be running Olympus.

Moving away from the steps to the balcony, Persephone could think of no way of getting the tart where she wanted her, until she remembered Hades' little pet.

She made her way into his pen and was greeted by growls and snarls. The puppy had never liked her, and the feeling was mutual, but he was a means to an end.

She would use Hades' favourite pet to help her get rid of the female.

If Persephone wanted Olympus, she needed the powers of the elder gods. The first god she would drain and remove was Hades, but to do that she needed, for starters, to get rid of the competition. She was prepared to sacrifice many a life to get what she wanted, and she always got her way.

Persephone ignored the harmless growls and snarls and stepped closer. Cerberus was all bark and definitely no bite. She had no idea why the god had adopted a pathetic creature like Cerberus, he made a useless guard dog.

Kneeling in front of the animal, Persephone smiled and was rewarded by the dog quietening down. Instead, it tilted its head from side to side, watching her, unsure of what she would do.

"That's a good doggy," she crooned, before she slid the blade of her dagger - the one she had killed the mortal female with - into its paw. With speed only a goddess possessed, she pulled it out and moved away from the now enraged and in pain animal. His snarls joined, this time, by whimpers. There had been a time when they would have pulled at her heart, but that had been the old Persephone, the one that loved animals and the beauty of life.

Apollo had taught her different, instilled in her that more can be gained by blood and pain, and it was a lifestyle she had fully embraced.

Persephone slipped into the shadows of the trees that surrounded the pen and was rewarded by her target investigating the loud whimpers that Cerberus was making. Anger filled her as she looked over the mortal. Yes, she was pretty, but not as beautiful as Persephone. Putting aside the fact she may have burnt her bridges with Hades a long time ago when she told him he was an ugly man and she would never be joined with him, why would a god turn down her for that? In hindsight, she could have been nicer, but she didn't want to be married to him because her mother said so.

But she wouldn't be deterred, all the elder gods would pay for their arrogance.

Stepping from the shadows, she called the female's name. She didn't expect much of a fight and revelled in the chance to spill more blood.

"Andromeda," she repeated, and smiled sweetly as the female turned, their eyes meeting. Persephone sauntered forward, not bothering to hide the small dagger she still held in her palm. The sooner the female knew her time was up, the easier it would be.

"Who are you?" she asked, and Persephone

watched as her eyes landed on the still-bloody dagger before she looked back at the oversized dog. "Why the fuck would you hurt an innocent animal?" Her voice was laced with anger, and that took Persephone by surprise. Most mortals quivered in fear at any of the gods, yet this female didn't. That would soon change.

"I do what I want, when I want. I don't have to explain myself to a pathetic mortal!"

Persephone stopped her approach only a few feet away from Andromeda, her body tingling with the excitement of what she was about to do.

Barbara – Barbie, to her friends - walked along the dirt path. She didn't know where she was or where she was going, but she knew she had to keep moving. There was pull deep down in her soul that told her to she was on the right path.

Her memory was a little fuzzy. She remembered being on a date with a gorgeous guy called Mett, and then he offered to walk her home.

She had been rather excited about that. The prospect of a kiss and maybe more had made her day.

But how she ended up on this path, she could quite remember.

The scenery around her - if she had been interested in such things - would have been perfect for someone to photograph. Beautiful trees covered in blossoms swayed in a gentle breeze, flowers in every colour of the rainbow doted small fields.

"Where am I?" she asked herself as she stopped and looked around. Seeing a small pond, she walked over and looked down into the crystal waters.

The reflection that looked back at her, wasn't her.

With gentle fingers, she touched her pale skin. Being a red-head, she knew she was pale, but this was deathly pale. Her hands shook as she looked down at herself, finally seeing what her mind had rebelled at.

Her clothes were the same ones she had worn for the date, only she was now sporting a large hole under the left side of her ribs. The clothing surrounding the area was still stained with blood.

Barbara cried out and fell to her knees as memories flooded her mind and system, sending her into a sobbing heap.

She was dead, her life taken by some jumped-up tart dressed like a Grecian hooker. Barbie felt angry and at the same time heartbroken. Her life had been taken before she had known love, before she had gotten married, had kids and really lived.

Ghostly tears fell freely from her eyes, staining her cheeks, until a light hand landed on her shoulder.

Another ghost - or soul - like her smiled down at her. Taking her hand, it helped her stand.

"Shhhh, it's ok. All will be ok."

With that, Barbara followed the ghost, letting her lead her to Elyssia.

Chapter Twenty-Four

Andromeda watched the slow approach of the woman in front of her. She was breathtakingly beautiful, yet there was something off about her. She was dressed in a sheer gown that consisted of browns and golds. Her long, dark hair fell past her waist, curling at the tips. Unfortunately, Andromeda could see what she had to offer; the woman's nipples could clearly be seen through the fabric, and it was obvious she didn't know what knickers were.

It was the woman's eyes that held Andromeda's attention though, captured it and worried her slightly. They were a deep, dark brown that, on any sane person, would be stunning. But hers held a hint of darkness, almost like she wasn't all there, focused yet distant. The coldness that she could practically feel resonating from her in waves and the way she held the sharp dagger had Andromeda scared. For a woman that would happily stab a creature like Cerberus… It made her wonder what else she was capable of.

"Who are you?" Andromeda repeated, and stepped back a little. The whimpers from Cerberus behind her had her reaching a hand out to place it on the snout of one of his heads. She stroked gently, although she never took her eyes off the woman.

"Oh, that's disappointing," she sneered, and twisted the dagger in her hand. Her eyes flickered as her head twitched a little. "I am Persephone, soon to be Queen of Olympus," she said, waving her arms.

Andromeda didn't know what she expected her to do with that information. She wasn't about to bow down, if that was what she wanted.

"To be queen, don't you have to be married to Zeus?" Andromeda questioned.

"You know nothing, mortal. Zeus won't be around much longer, and then I will be queen." Persephone spat out, and Andromeda saw the change in the goddess. Her eyes twitched even more as she started to ramble. The goddess started to pace in front of her, waving her hands and using the dagger to annunciate her ramblings.

"All I have to do is get rid of the elder gods, then I

can have their powers and rule Olympus like I was born to do. Zeus will be easy once I have stolen the powers from his brother. Poseidon may be a little difficult but…" she continued her fervid speech, and Andromeda pretended to listen as slowly edged away. She needed to escape and warn Hades, warn anyone that Persephone had lost it. Her brain was unstable and she was about to lose her shit completely.

Andromeda had no idea if her hare-brained plan would work - she didn't know the rules of Olympus - but one thing was for sure: she wouldn't be getting anywhere near Cerberus. Hell, Andromeda was an absolute pussy most of the time, but there was no way this fruit loop was ever hurting Cerberus again. Andromeda had never been a confrontational person - she would much rather walk out and leave than get into a fight with someone.

But this was different. Something deep inside Andromeda refused to run from this woman, refused to be the coward she always felt herself to be. It could have been the way she had stabbed Cerberus with no remorse that had changed the way she felt, or it could have been the threat to Hades.

"You are fucking batshit, woman," Andromeda snapped, pulling Persephone from her ranting and pacing. She soon realised that may not have been the best thing to say to someone not only wielding a dagger like a composer's baton but slowly losing her marbles.

Instead of answering, Persephone grinned. It wasn't a happy grin, it was a bone-chilling, evil clown grin that sent shivers up and down Andromeda's spine and turned her stomach.

"You have a mouth on you, just like your mortal bitch friend," she sneered. "I soon shut her up, just as I will you." The goddess slowly stalked forward, causing Andromeda to back up, step for step.

"Hades won't be able to resist me once you're out of the way." She laughed, and the sound felt cold and dead.

"What did you do to Barbara?" Andromeda snapped, her heart racing and pumping blood until it sounded in her head. The pain those simple words had caused felt like a lead weight on her whole body. Barbie had been the only friend she could turn to - her best friend.

Persephone laughed again and flicked the dagger in her hand, fresh and old blood could be seen on the blade. "I simply shut her up. She was annoying me." The goddess shrugged.

"You killed her?" Andromeda shouted. "You

killed my best friend?" Andromeda didn't fight the tears as they erupted from her eyes and cascaded down her cheeks.

"Yes," Persephone said calmly. "Yes, I did."

"You psycho cow!" Andromeda whispered vehemently. "You won't win."

"Ha! that's what you think, little mortal, but now it's your turn." The goddess palmed the handle of the dagger and moved towards Andromeda. The glint of the blade with her friend's blood on urged her into action. She picked up the edge of the robe she wore and ran back towards the entrance to the pen and through the garden. Her feet made little noise on the cool grass as she moved past the crystal stream. Andromeda sneaked a look behind her. Seeing no goddess, she frowned.

The goddess had been right behind her, looking like a villain from a horror movie, her eyes all crazy. She was like a real-life version of Druzella from Buffy, and Andromeda wanted to be as far away as possible.

As she moved past a tree, she didn't see the figure waiting for her until it was too late. She felt something slam into her chest. Her feet stopped moving and she looked down to see only the hilt remaining, the rest of the blade buried in her heart.

"You can't run from a goddess, super powers and

all that," Persephone sneered as she stood in front of Andromeda, watching as she slowly sunk to her knees. Andromeda felt the cool grass against her skin as her lifeblood seeped out from the wound. Only the feet of the goddess could now be seen. Andromeda lay still, her mind not wanting to admit that this was it for her. She would never again see her mother or her best friend. She wouldn't see Hades. She thought about the possibility of getting reborn again, but she didn't want to lose all her memories, the ones she had with him and the new ones she had gained from past lives. It felt like this had been her last chance and she would now fade into oblivion, given no more chances to live in the mortal world again. Tears coursed down her face as her breaths became shallow, her lungs fighting for breath as her heart fought for each beat. She brought Hades' kind face to mind, picturing the smile he had given her as they'd made love for the first time, and how it felt to be wrapped in his arms. Only, the words of the Persephone took that peace from her, bringing her back to reality.

"Goodbye, mortal. You were never worthy." The goddess laughed, its sound cruel, before she walked away, leaving Andromeda lying in a pool of her cooling blood.

"I love you, Hades," she whispered as she watched the bare feet of the goddess vanish. She took one last faltering breath, and then no more.

Chapter Twenty-Five

Hades burst into his room only to find Andromeda missing from his bed. Calling on his servants, he investigated the bathroom before heading out onto the balcony.

Still no sign.

His heart erupted in his chest, thumping against his ribcage as if it would burst, the words of the fates repeating in his mind over and over.

"Her life is already forfeit."

No, it wasn't. They didn't control his fate anymore. No one did but him.

"Andromeda," he shouted, hearing his voice echo off the marble. "Andromeda," he repeated, desperate to hear her voice shout back. Hades strained his ears to listen, but the only noises he heard where the gentle trickle of the stream in his garden. Moving down the steps, Hades walked onto the grass, his large feet making the leaves crunch.

"Andromeda," he called out again, frustration eating at him. Where was she, why would she leave him after what they had shared the night before? He had felt whole for the first time in his life, and she had said as much to him.

A quiet whimper sounded from within the garden, and his feet smacked against the ground as he took off on a run. Passing the flowers he had planted for his mate, he stumbled to a stop by the stream.

Cerberus, his guardian and friend, lay on the grass, but not in his pen. His whimpers grew louder and louder as Hades approached.

"Cerberus," Hades called out, and one of the heads turned to look at him, his eyes full of sadness and moisture. "What is it boy?"

As the other two heads lifted, revealing their prize, Hades fell to his knees.

His world came crashing down.

His hands found her hair first. She hadn't put it back into a braid, instead leaving it loose, the colour still as beautiful as the day he had first seen her. He leant forward, his hands stroking her face, feeling her cold skin before he lifted her and brought Andromeda to his chest.

Tears fell down Hades' cheeks as he pressed her to his chest. His lips kissed her head as he rocked, with only the sound of Cerberus whining to keep him company. Andromeda, his mate, was dead, and there was nothing he, as an immortal, could do to change that. With all of his powers - his immortal skills - he couldn't bring back the one person that meant more than life itself.

Holding her in his arms, Hades looked down at her, then gently brushed her cheeks, moving her hair away from her face so he could see her better. Her lashes rested on her cheeks as if she was sleeping, yet he would never see her pale eyes look at him again, never hear his name on her lips that instead of a plump pink now looked blue. Resting his own cheek against hers, he continued to rock her. The tears wouldn't stop, and he didn't want them to. His heart was gone. It had been hers for centuries, and now his heart was gone.

Hades looked down at Andromeda's still form to where Cerberus rested his three heads. Every now and again, one would nudge her bare foot in the hope she would show him attention. Hades felt the same. He would give anything to have her say his name.

Hades' eyes focused on the dagger that was still embedded in her chest, the jewelled hilt reflecting in the dull light. A spark of recognition blossomed, and he reached forward and gently removed the cause of his grief. A simple weapon that had taken everything from him, and he knew who the owner was.

Grief was replaced quickly by anger. The grief fuelled it, helped increase its potency, and as Hades collected Andromeda into his arms, he lifted his head to the sky of his home and roared that grief, roared so loud that even Olympus herself would hear the pain and anguish.

Servants lined his path as Hades carried Andromeda back into his temple. All bowed their heads in respect. They had known who she was the minute he had brought her home, her soul recognisable even though her form was different. Hades had looked at every one of them, hoping to see her so he knew she would be reborn, but this time was different. They had run out of time, his mate would not be offered the chance to return to the mortal world.

Stepping into his bedroom, Hades growled. Perched on the small table in his room was Persephone.

"Hello, handsome," she purred, not even reacting to the fact he was carrying a dead mortal in his arms. He had known it was her the moment he had seen the dagger. Persephone, over the years, had become rather fond of jewelled items and had commission his own metal smiths to make such pieces. She arrogantly would have an elaborate 'P' decorated on them.

The dagger that had killed his mate had such a mark.

Ignoring Persephone and her draped position over the table, he walked over to his bed and placed Andromeda down, taking his time to move her hands over her stomach as well as rearranging her hair so it framed her face. Here she looked at beautiful and at peace. Hades leaned down and kissed her lips before he stood and faced the goddess.

"What do you want, Persephone?" he sneered out.

"Oh, is your mortal… dead? That's a pity," she commented, and it made Hades' blood boil, but he stayed silent and instead folded his arms over his chest.

"I wanted to come and see you. We need to talk about our arrangement," she said sweetly, and moved from her perched position, her bare feet travelling silently towards him, but still Hades kept quiet.

"You know, the one where we get married," she purred, and stroked his bicep. Hades felt repulsed by her touch. He only wanted one woman's touch, and she lay in the bed behind him, dead.

"No," was all he said.

"What do you mean no?" He watched as her eyes

shifted and revealed a madness Hades had never noticed before.

"I mean, no, I won't marry you. To be frank, Persephone, I don't like you." He answered as honestly as he could and was rewarded by the widening of her eyes. The hand on his bicep curled and her nails dug into his flesh.

"You arrogant son of a-"

"Shut up, Persephone," he growled. Shaking off her arm, he turned and once again looked down at Andromeda. The empty space where his heart had been, hurt, a pain like one hundred daggers digging in and twisting.

"Oh, come on, Hades. What does one pathetic mortal's life matter? Get over her already. You are a god, after all."

The words hit Hades' ears and were slow to filter in, but as they did, Hades felt his own power surge, the grief and anger combining and taking over. In one fluid motion, he turned, grabbing the goddess by the neck and lifting her into the air, his roar filling not only the temple but the whole of Elyssia itself.

"SHUT THE FUCK UP!" Persephone's eyes widened in shock as he tightened his hold. "I know it was you, goddess," he growled and tightened further. "You come to my home, injure my charge, and then murder *my soulmate.*" His voice caused the temple itself to shake.

Persephone choked as Hades continued to squeeze her throat, slowly cutting off her airway. She couldn't be killed this way, but it would shut her up and given him a tiny bit of release for his grief. He would rip her head off, clean from her shoulders. That thought passed through his head multiple times. She deserved a fate much worse for what she had done.

"Hades?" a deep voice sounded from behind.

"Hades?" another softer voice joined the first, calling him out of his grief-stricken haze.

Chapter Twenty-Six

Aphrodite's heart hurt. Whose wouldn't when you saw the pure emotion flowing from Hades? Everything had been going so well, she had felt it in the energies, and then nothing. It had been like a light had turned off and left nothing but darkness behind. Her eyes flickered over to where Hades had laid his mate, the blood-soaked clothing showing how she had died. She could feel Hades' pain as if it were her own, so she embraced it and let the tears flow.

Laying her hand on Hades' arm, she looked up into his face.

"Hades, put her down, this won't bring her back."

"Please, brother," Zeus called out, his own throat thick with emotion. All of Olympus had known something had happened, the very earth itself had shook with the power Hades gave off in his grief.

And to find out one of their own had been responsible, yet again, was a shock to the system. First

Apollo and now Persephone. Aphrodite looked to Zeus just as he gazed at her. Something was seriously wrong in Olympus, and it needed sorting before their entire world imploded on itself.

"She killed her," Hades croaked out as he dropped Persephone, letting her collapse to the floor at his feet. "She killed her," he repeated, ignoring her choking form as he moved back to the bed, sitting on the edge and taking Andromeda's hands in his own.

"She killed her," he whispered, and Aphrodite witnessed the god of the underworld lose himself to the pain of a broken heart.

The goddess of love looked again to Zeus and he nodded. Persephone needed to be punished, but not the same as Apollo. He would be dealt with in due time for his involvement in this and what had happened with Cupid. But murder of an innocent within Elyssia itself… To murder a mortal under the direct protection of the god of the underworld was punishable by death.

Aphrodite felt nothing as she looked upon Persephone. She used to be a beautifully kind goddess, but then she had become involved with Apollo and his twisted ways. He had assisted in the destruction of an innocent soul.

"Persephone," Aphrodite called as she knelt next to the breathless goddess. "How could you?"

"Oh, fuck off," Persephone spat, and gripped her neck, slowly getting to her feet. "You were always Miss. Goody Goody, too fucking weak and nice to take what you want."

Persephone grinned. "That's why I took what you wanted instead." She laughed and looked around her, her eyes flickering. "He thought I wouldn't be able to tell who he was, but no one can mistake your tell-tale signature, Aphrodite. It floated around him like a foul stench."

Aphrodite stood, still from shock. Meton was no longer missing, Persephone had been the one to take him. Which also meant he wasn't responsible for the mortal's death either.

"You have him? Where?" Aphrodite asked, desperation eating into her voice.

"Fuck you," Persephone spat out. "Fuck all of you."

"SILENCE." Zeus's voice rang out, making the temple shake, and Aphrodite bowed her head in respect as Zeus stalked to a still defiant Persephone. Her face showed her hate, and she lifted her chin.

"Persephone, your mother has asked that I be lenient on you. Although she doesn't know the full extent of your warped actions" Persephone grinned at this and Aphrodite had the urge to smack her in the face. She wasn't prone to violence, but something about the other goddess ticked her off.

The gentle footsteps of Demeter pulled Aphrodite's gaze from Persephone. The elder goddess looked sad yet resigned.

"Persephone," she called. "Daughter" she whispered.

"Mother, tell them to release me," Persephone demanded, but was only rewarded by a shake of the head from her mother.

"I, Demeter, hereby renounce you, Persephone, as my daughter." she calmly stated before she looked at Zeus and nodded her head. What more could she do? Her daughter had stepped over a line and then some. Aphrodite didn't miss the tears that erupted from Demeter's eyes as she turned away and left the room.

Now it was up to Zeus.

"But, I'm afraid for the death of not one but two mortals under the direct protection of Hades, the lord and god of the underworld, as well as committing murder in Elyssia itself and kidnapping a goddess's companion, you are sentenced to banishment."

Persephone still grinned, but that soon vanished

as Zeus raised his hands. Using his power, he pushed her back until she hit the wall of marble.

"What? I thought I was being banished, what are you doing?" she screeched, and Aphrodite had no sympathy for what was to come.

"Persephone," Zeus announced as he approached, his large hand reaching out and pressing against her chest. "I banish your soul for all eternity." His hand disappeared inside her chest, and light erupted as he slowly withdrew, clutching her soul. What used to be a bright light was now tinged with greys and black, showing just how corrupt and evil she had become.

"I, Zeus, banish your soul to the depths of Tartarus, where only the demons will keep you company. You will never be free. This is your sentence, so be it."

Aphrodite watched the ball that was the soul of Persephone as it vanished, Zeus's sentence reinforced by the magic of the gods. Persephone's body, still pinned to the wall, dropped lifelessly to the floor. An empty shell.

"Zeus," the goddess of love called out, "take Hades to Olympus and stay with him. I have work to do here."

She looked from the body of Persephone to that of Andromeda, an idea forming in her head, one that would need the consent of all elder gods. Although, she already knew Hades' answer. As if reading her mind, Zeus nodded before moving to his brother. In a flash of light, she was left alone.

Love still had work to do, and time was not her friend if she wanted to help Hades and save her companion.

Chapter Twenty-Seven

Andromeda felt light, like that feeling when you've had some good painkillers and they kick in on an empty stomach. She usually liked the feeling, but this time it felt strange, especially when she couldn't remember taking any painkillers at all.

Her last memory had been of pain and anguish. Her heart had hurt.

She had been stabbed, but that wasn't why it had hurt.

Hades...

His name whispered across her mind like a gentle caress, and she forced her eyes open. He was the reason her heart had hurt. She knew she wouldn't see him again.

Lifting her head, she found herself on Hades' bed, back in the beautifully elaborate room she loved and reminded her of him.

"Hello, Andromeda." A soft voice pulled her gaze

to a chair placed by her beside. Turning, she saw a beautiful female, this one had golden blonde hair and violet eyes that, instead of being crazy, were kind.

"How do you know my name? What happened? Wasn't I dead?"

"My name is Aphrodite." The female waited and Andromeda nodded, showing she recognised the name. "And yes, you had died."

"So, how am I here?" Andromeda asked as she slowly sat herself up, stilling as she noticed the material she was dressed in. A gown of deep blue covered her. Laced with silver, it sparkled like the stars in Elyssia. Picking up the material, Andromeda felt it between her fingers, loving the feel of the silk and chiffon.

"That's difficult to explain," Aphrodite answered, and stood before walking around the bed to stand in front of a full-length mirror, its frame a mix of fruits and leaves, all made in silver. It had been covered by a blue curtain when Andromeda had been in the bedroom before.

Aphrodite held out her hand in invitation to Andromeda. "Come stand by me and let me show you instead."

Getting to her feet, Andromeda felt a little unsteady, her head spun but it quickly wore off as she walked towards the goddess. Taking her hand, she smiled and then, at Aphrodite's request, looked into the mirror.

"What the ever-loving fuck!"

"Ha! That's what I said when I first saw you," a familiar voice said, followed by the form of Andromeda's best friend, Barbie, who stood behind her.

"Oh, Barbie! I'm sorry," Andromeda cried, and turned to hug her friend, only for her arms to pass straight through her.

"Nice try, tart, but I'm a ghost, no hugs allowed."

"Technically you are a soul, not a ghost, Barbara," Aphrodite corrected, and received a roll of the eyes from the now bodiless Barbie.

"As I said, I was dubious about the new look, but if you study yourself closely, you can see that you're not the same."

Andromeda once again turned to the mirror and stepped closer. On a brief glance, she was the goddess Persephone, only on closer inspection you could see the subtle differences. Instead of dark brown eyes, hers were now an amber. Her hair was no longer a delicious brown. Instead, it was lighter; streaks of white and gold covered it, making it completely different to the previous owner.

"What did you do?" Andromeda asked, turning to the goddess.

"I made you a goddess, Andromeda. We had Persephone banished for her crimes, but her body had been left behind - a healthy, immortal body. Your soul had not made its way to Elyssia yet, and if I'm frank, I don't think it *would* have made it. As you have become aware, your soul has lived many times, and as such, had reached the end of its journey." Aphrodite sighed and took Andromeda's hands in her own. "I did what I could for love. Now, I know the form is not a happy memory for you, but it was my only option. I couldn't let the chance for Hades to have his soulmate pass me by. Zeus agreed and gave me the go ahead."

Andromeda nodded and looked again at the mirror, turning this way and that, getting used to the new body. She felt curvier than her old body had been, and more well-endowed in the breast area. Pulling the top out, she looked into it.

"Barbie! I've finally got bigger tits than you." Andromeda laughed and grinned at her best friend, only to get the finger in return.

"Is there not a body we can find for Barbara?"

Aphrodite shook her head. "I'm sorry, no. An immortal body with no soul is a rare thing indeed."

"Whoa, whoa, whoa, hold it there, twinkle toes," Barbie shouted, and stepped in front of Andromeda. "Yes, I am dead, it sucks balls, and I wanted to get married and all that jazz, but love over here said I could stay down here and help you if I wanted, or I could go drink from the river over there. I choose you, bestie, always will. Plus, do I look like I wanna drink from a damn river? Ugh, no thank you."

"Oh, tart, I love you." Andromeda started to cry.

"I love you, too, Rommie. Now stop crying, tie up your hair, and go get your man. I think that body and new titties needs breaking in." Andromeda laughed as Barbie winked, turned, and walked out of the room. She could hear her barking orders at the servants as she went, only to be stopped short by Aphrodite.

"Barbara," the goddess called out, and waited for her to turn around. "I have to ask…" Andromeda was shocked at the sadness in her eyes, "Do you have any idea where Meton is?"

"Meton?" Barbara questioned, and then realised who she was asking about. Shaking her head, she responded, "I'm sorry, goddess, I was dead before that nutjob took him. I'm so sorry."

Andromeda watched as Aphrodite nodded her thanks and took a deep breath, almost like she was steeling herself, boarding up her feelings. When she had turned back to face Andromeda, she had a smile in place.

"Thank you, Aphrodite, for everything."

Aphrodite nodded. "My pleasure. Now, please do as your friend insists; go to Hades. Show him life is worth it, show him love is worth waiting and fighting for."

"Where is he?" she asked, her hands taking her new, long hair and working it into her signature braid.

"He's by your grave," Aphrodite answered, and Andromeda froze.

"My grave?"

"Yes, in the garden." Aphrodite stood back, quickly vanishing in a flash of light, her whispered words of good luck lingering in the air.

Chapter Twenty-Eight

Hades sat in the grass of his private garden and watched the stream flow by. Not long after he had returned from Zeus's temple, he had been asked by Aphrodite if he wanted Andromeda's body to bury or burn. To send it back to the mortal world now would have been disrespectful to her memory and would have caused too much of an issue with the authorities.

So, instead, he had brought her to his garden and laid her to rest underneath the cherry blossom tree. At least here he could sit and, in a way, talk to her. He hadn't seen her soul on the Elyssian fields, although he had looked. He just hoped with everything he had that she had finally found peace.

It hurt to think that less than twenty-four hours ago she had been with him, in his bed, and had accepted who and what he was. He would always remember the feel of her in his arms, the touch of his lips on hers, and her voice in his ears calling his name.

They were all he had left to keep him company for the rest of his days.

Flicking a piece of grass from his jeans, Hades closed his eyes and rested his head back against the tree. He listened to the sound of the water and appreciated the quiet breeze as it whispered through the leaves.

"Hades," a soft voice called out, one that held a trace of familiarity. He ignored it, hoping that, whoever it was, would take the hint and leave him alone.

"Hades…" The voice was closer still.

Keeping his eyes closed, he responded, "Go away." He was in no mood for company.

A soft hand touched his shoulder. Hades grabbed at it and brought the owner over his shoulder and into his lap.

"I said…" His words stopped and his hand automatically went to the throat of the woman now sprawled in his lap. He watched as she fought the grip, her eyes wide with fear. He had been assured that Persephone was gone, but here she was, taunting him with her presence.

"I should kill you," he growled out and squeezed.

The more he looked, though, the more he doubted his actions. Instead of chocolate-brown eyes, golden amber ones looked up at him, pleading for him to let her go. Her hair was not the dark colour he remembered either, it was now a stunning combination of whites, golds, and browns.

He again looked into her eyes, and saw no evil. Instead, he saw acceptance and love. Her scent carried across his nose and brought with it memories of his mate. Hades frowned as he released her neck.

"Who are you?" he asked, letting her crawl from his lap and rub her neck. The dress she wore was also not something the goddess would have favoured. By contrast, it matched his usual robes.

"Tell me who you are," he demanded.

The female watched him before she sat back on her heels.

"Am I that different from before, Hades?" she asked. "You've loved me in all my forms, can't you love me in this one as well?"

The words had only just made it out of her mouth before she was back on Hades' lap and in his arms. His rough hands stroked her cheek before one tugged on her signature braid.

"Andromeda…" he breathed. "How?" he asked, his voice choked with emotion.

"Aphrodite," she answered, and that was all the explanation needed. Hades would thank the goddess later, but for now, he had his own goddess to worship. Rolling her underneath him and onto the grass, he framed her face with his hands, his thumbs stroking her cheeks.

She was right: he would love her no matter what form she took. She was his soulmate, the owner of his heart, and his queen.

Aphrodite had called it all that time ago.

Love does, in fact, always find a way, and now even the lord of the dead had his lady.

Epilogue

Aphrodite had a headache, one of those ones that hits you right behind the eyes and makes you see colours. Most were caused by weather changes or even just lack of sleep. If only her cause was as easy to deal with.

The catalysts for her current sore head stood in front of each other. No words had been exchanged, just glares and daggers and whatever else you would like to call the dirty looks.

Hera and Zeus had been pissed at each other for as long as Aphrodite could remember. Only, she couldn't recall the exact cause. No one could. There had been rumours - lots of those had gone around - stating that Zeus was unable to stay faithful to his wife, and that Hera had refused Zeus and would not let him near her. So, time had passed and things between them had only grown more and more sour.

On the surface, it was easy to think that they

hated each other with a passion. Only those, like Aphrodite, knew what lay hidden just beneath the surface. Love, raw and untamed.

Those two loved each other with every part of their godly souls, but they had lost trust and respect for each other. Instead of listening to their hearts, they had listened to the rumours that had been made up just to divide them, and they had let it happen. When they had first wed, Olympus had been in its youth. They were both fresh and young, eager to be what the mortals needed them to be. Only, some had been jealous of Zeus, and even of Hera, for she was chosen to rule by his side.

Aphrodite shook her head. Jealousy: the root cause for a lot of issues. Apollo, Hera, Zeus, and even Hades had suffered a little bit with it. But, she smiled, but love had won out, as it always did.

Now here she sat with the headache that could have been dragged from the underworld, watching the king of Olympus have a stare down with his wife. She rolled her eyes, this was not going to be easy or fun, but something had to give. Olympus could not survive if they continued the path they were on, which meant this whole rift needed fixing.

So, she had summoned Poseidon and Hades to help as well as Hermes, for only they could aid her with what she had planned. However, she may actually lose her friend in Hera if she went through with it. But the greater good came first.

"Ahhh, still fighting, I see. Weren't they doing that the last time I was here?" Poseidon's deep, throaty voice announced as he strolled into the room. Aphrodite blinked rapidly. The last time she had seen the god of the sea, he had been traditionally dressed, but now… She tilted her head. Now he looked good, wearing cut-off jeans that reached his knees and a top that showed off his powerful arms.

"It's a tank top, and yes, he looks hot."

Aphrodite turned her head and smiled at the new and improved Persephone, although no one called her by that name. She was still Andromeda to everyone, and with a new soul inside what was a body used for evil, she was a breath of fresh air to the realm. And also brought a little mortal to it all as well.

"He does indeed," Aphrodite breathed.

"Hey." Hades frowned over at them as he walked passed, but there was no anger in his eyes. They only held the love and devotion he felt for his soulmate.

Aphrodite and Andromeda giggled, and they both sighed as they watched the big, bad three clasp hands. All were tall and powerfully built gods. It was easy to see why so many would fall under their spell.

"Why am I here?" Hera called out, silencing the room. Her voice was slightly raised and her body posture showed she was annoyed. Although, to Aphrodite, she could see she was on the verge of tears.

"Ok, thank you for coming. I've called you all here because we have to deal with an important matter."

"Who died and made you leader?" Hera sneered, and Aphrodite frowned. They had been close friends once, until Hera had pushed everyone away.

"Hera!" Zeus chastised.

"Don't talk to me," Hera snapped at Zeus.

Aphrodite stood and walked towards the group. She was starting to get annoyed now.

"Ok, the issue we have - and by we, I mean the whole of bloody Olympus - is with you two." She looked at both Hera and Zeus, waving her fingers at them. "Your fighting is starting to affect us all. If we want to survive, you two need to cut it out."

"How can I when all he has done is lie to me, cheat on me? I don't want to sort things out. I want a divorce."

"Fuck that, Hera. You are my wife. If you would just listen for a fucking minute… But no, you have to believe what all your little buddies say."

"That's it!" Aphrodite yelled. "I've fucking had it.

Poseidon, Hades, if you could assist me, I would be most grateful."

"Of course, goddess." They both answered with grins, glad to help sort something that had been bothering nearly every immortal. At the same time, they raised their hands, summoning their powers.

"As love commands, I banish you both. You will not return until you have learned to trust and love one another, as know you should, deep in your soul."

"You cannot banish us!"

Aphrodite ignored Hera's outraged cry and continued with her spell. "Return only when love is true. I banish you to the mortal realm. May love protect you,"

Before a blinding flash of light engulfed the couple, Aphrodite saw the shocked look on both their faces. As much as they would hate her now, this was for the best.

"Where did you send them?" Hades asked as he walked over to his mate and wrapped her in his arms.

"Blackpool, England."

A snort followed by laughter filled the room as Hermes and Andromeda reacted to the news.

"Why Blackpool?"

"Sonia said it would be a good place to send them, she didn't say why."

"Oh, that's brilliant." Hermes wiped the tears from his eyes as he leaned on his staff.

"Laugh it up, messenger boy." Hades smirked and smacked Hermes on the back. "You're on babysitting duty."

"What?"

"He's correct, Hermes. I need you there with them to keep an eye on things. They won't have their godly powers and will have to act like mortals. They are going to need your guidance."

"Oh, for fuck sake." The pouty look on Hermes' face made Aphrodite giggle.

"This is for the greater good, Hermes."

"Yeah, yeah. What the fuck ever," Hermes grumbled. "You guys' owe me." With that, he changed into his winged form, leaving the room quickly.

"Well, this should be fun to watch." Andromeda laughed as she moved across the temple, still wrapped in Hades' arms. They tightened a little, securing her at his side as he bent his head and kissed the top of hers.

"Let's go home, my love," he answered, but turned his head towards Aphrodite. "Tell Cupid I haven't forgotten." With that, he smiled at Aphrodite a moment before they, too, vanished.

"You need anything else, goddess?" Poseidon had remained and watched her carefully. His eyes, the same turquoise of the Mediterranean, seemed to miss nothing. She shook her head, her thoughts turning to her missing companion.

"No, not at this time. Thank you for your help, Poseidon. I know leaving your realm makes you uncomfortable."

She watched as he smiled then bowed. "Anything for the goddess of love."

With those simple words, he, too, changed form, his body vanishing into a mist that held every colour of the rainbow. It hung in the air before it moved out of the temple, leaving Aphrodite alone.

Exhausted, she dropped into a chair and closed her eyes. Being love wasn't easy, but it was all she knew. Only time would now tell if her interference would make any difference.

Love was hard, it was cruel and unyielding, yet it was breathtakingly beautiful. Through it all, love was soul-shatteringly worth it.

THE END

Acknowledgements

Book number six.

That alone makes me think holy crap. I have a mixture of feelings, Fear, elation, pride.
I couldn't have done this without the following people.
So here's huge Dolly thank you to:

Mandy Barker and Yericka Aviles, without you guys I would have gone batshit crazy. You help keep me grounded even when my characters go on bender.

Steph aka wench, aka tart aka my editor, who not only gets me, understands every typo I make but outs in all nighters for me. You woman are amazing and thank you for putting up with me. Love your face.

The three stooges or the three musketeers Annie,

Mich and Tammy. My world would definitely not be as awesome as it is now with you guys in it. I would be lost without your honesty and support.

Jada D'Lee for my third amazing cover in the soulmate series, this lady is one gifted wench and knows exactly what I need for this series. As the creator of the covers for the soulmate series there would be no one else I trusted. Thank you Jada.

The graphics Shed for once again doing an awesome job formatting and getting my doc ready for the world to see.

My Chapter chicks, I love you ladies so much and thank you for your continued support.

And finally…. To all of my amazing readers that support every single story I release, that want my words and make this whole journey an amazing one. I would be lost without you all.

Thank you from the bottom of my heart.

Jenn xx

A Note From Jenn

Do you want more from J Thompson?

SoulKiss Book 1 Soulmate Series
SoulFate Book 2 Soulmate Series

Exercise in Love (stand alone)

Cupids Essence (Soulmate Series Spin off)

Dark Confusion (dark Desire Book 1)

Also keep a look out for

Ebony (Trinity Series Book 1)

Dark Need (Dark Desire Book 2)

Coming 2018

www.ingramcontent.com/pod-product-compliance
Ingram Content Group UK Ltd.
Pitfield, Milton Keynes, MK11 3LW, UK
UKHW022210230426
12048UKWH00016BA/748